Mal

and t

Cloud-Stealer

"That's right," Malcolm said, going to the door and staring gloomily out. "I just wish we knew what was happening. I wish another bird would come along and tell us what's going on in that Hidden Valley, and where Colcozzen is."

"If that 'awk was still around," Smudge said, "you could ask 'im to go 'ave a look."

Malcolm turned, looking at Smudge with a strange look in his eyes. "I don't think I need the hawk."

"Don't look at me!" Smudge said, flaring his wings nervously. "I ain't a carrier pigeon!"

"No," Malcolm said, the strange look in his eyes growing stronger. "I was thinking more of … going to the Valley myself."

Other titles in the Hippo Fantasy series:

The Night of Wishes
Michael Ende

The Wednesday Wizard
Sherryl Jordan

Ratspell
Paddy Mounter

Rowan of Rin
Emily Rodda

The Practical Princess and other Liberating Fairy Tales
Jay Williams

Look out for:

The Crystal Keeper
Jamie Jauncey

Rowan and the Travellers
Emily Rodda

Hippo Fantasy

Malcolm and the Cloud-Stealer

Douglas Hill

Scholastic Children's Books
7–9 Pratt Street, London NW1 0AE, UK
a division of Scholastic Publications Ltd
London ~ New York ~ Toronto ~ Sydney ~ Auckland

Published in the UK by Scholastic Publications Ltd, 1995

ISBN 0 590 55917 6

Typeset by TW Typesetting, Midsomer Norton, Avon

Printed by Cox & Wyman Ltd, Reading, Berks.

10 9 8 7 6 5 4 3 2 1

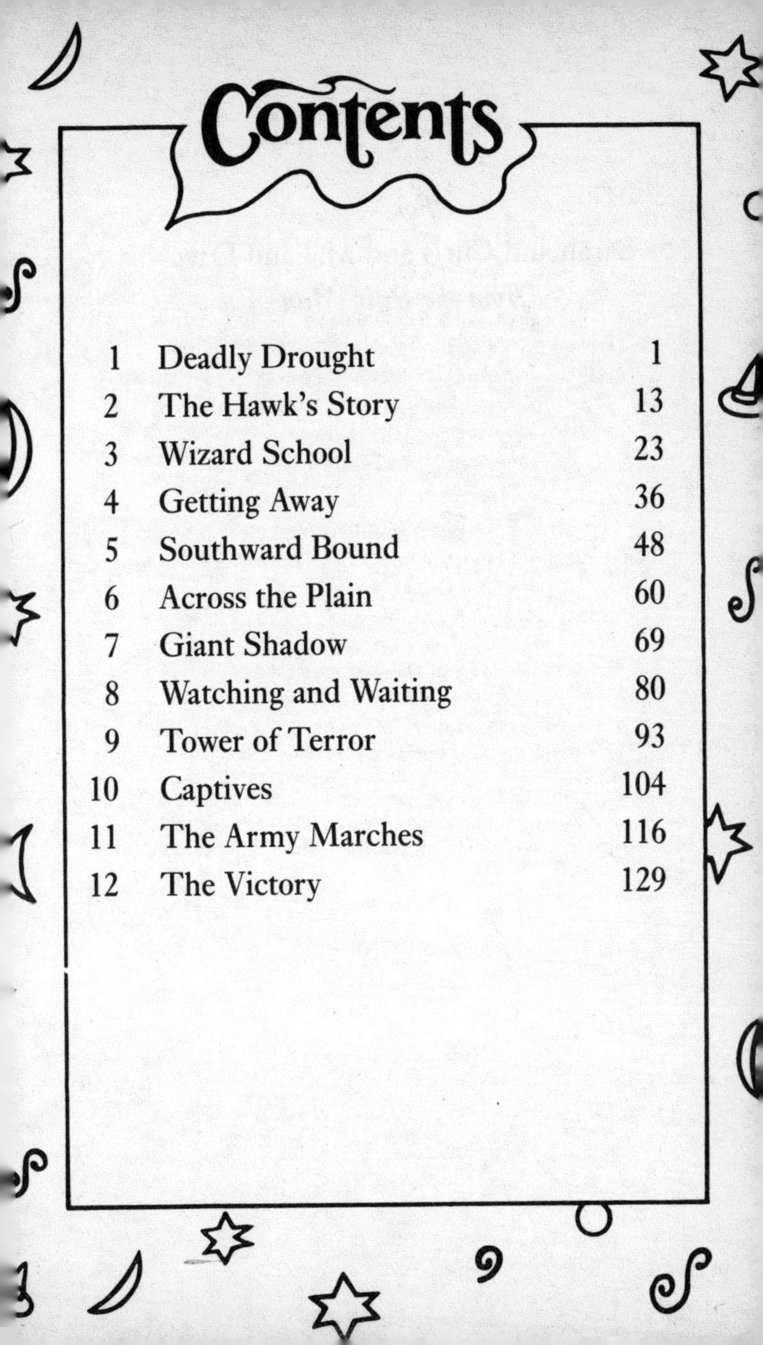

Contents

For

Sarah and Chris and Mal and Dave

from the Rain Man

Chapter 1

Deadly Drought

It was far too hot, Malcolm decided, to cook anything for breakfast. He sat limply at the table, feeling as if he was going to melt, nibbling on a piece of bread and sometimes fanning himself with it.

"Mornin', Malc!" said his friend Smudge, coming in through the open window. "'Ot, innit?"

"Too hot," Malcolm said crossly. "I'm sick of it."

"'Oo ain't?" Smudge said, settling on the windowsill. "'Ere – all yer tomato plants 'ave gone an' dried up an' died. You'll 'ave to grow some more if you want tomatoes to eat today."

Malcolm, who liked tomatoes, sighed. "I suppose I will."

Neither of them seemed to think it was at all odd, or unlikely, that Malcolm would be able to grow more tomatoes, ready to eat, in just one day.

"Wot's for breakfast?" Smudge wanted to know.

Malcolm waved a hand at the table-top. "You can have these breadcrumbs, if you like."

"Cheers," Smudge said, and fluttered over to the table.

He could do that because he was in fact a small, grey pigeon. And again, neither of them seemed to think it was at all odd or unlikely that a person and a pigeon should be chatting together.

But then, for Malcolm, talking to birds and growing plants quickly were perfectly normal things to do. Because he was *magical.*

Not that anyone would have guessed it from looking at him. He seemed very ordinary – a thin, rather quiet young man whose lanky arms and legs seemed a bit too long for his shirt and trousers. His straw-coloured hair stuck out untidily here and there, and his ears stuck out a bit as well. He was definitely not what anyone would expect a wizard or a sorcerer to look like.

But then, Malcolm wasn't really a wizard or a sorcerer. He simply had his own, special, rather small magic. Or, actually, *two* magics. He was able to talk to other living creatures – animals, birds, insects, anything. And he could make plants grow at amazing speed – any sort of plants, from any sort of soil, or from places where there was no soil at all.

Malcolm knew that his two magics were not very powerful or impressive. Certainly they hadn't been enough to get him into Wizard School when he was younger. All the same, he was very glad to have them. He enjoyed being able to talk to other creatures and to grow plants.

Also, his magic meant that he would never be poor or go hungry. His cow gave gallons of milk and his hens laid dozens of eggs, because he asked them to, nicely. And his garden was huge and overflowing because he could grow any plants that he wished, as many as he wished. So he was able to sell his extra milk and eggs and vegetables at the market in the nearby village, and use the money to buy other things that he needed.

Thanks to his two small magics, then, Malcolm's life was mostly quite comfortable, in a quiet and simple way. But it was also because of his magic that, some of the time, his life was a bit lonely.

His little cottage stood all by itself on the road to the village. In earlier years, Malcolm had lived there with his grandmother, who had brought him up, but now that she was gone he lived there alone, except for his hens, his cow and Smudge. He knew most of the people in the village and on the farms around the district, but he wasn't really friendly with them. He hardly ever had visitors or went visiting.

The other people weren't rude or unkind to him, but they were never very warm or welcoming. They treated him more like a stranger, keeping their distance – because, as Malcolm knew, they thought there was something strange about him.

And of course, in a way, they were right. He had always been a bit shy about telling people that he was magical, but they all knew that he was somehow different. Some of them thought he was slightly mad. After all, he lived alone and went everywhere with a pigeon on his shoulder.

Perhaps people had heard him talking to the pigeon, or to other birds and animals. Perhaps he had been seen around the countryside at night, when he had gone out to ask the local rabbits – nicely – not to eat his vegetables, or to ask the foxes to leave his hens alone. In any case, most people in the district thought that he was at least fairly peculiar, and so they mostly left him alone.

Malcolm had no idea how he could change the way the others treated him, if it could be changed at all. So he just put up with the fact that, now and then, he felt a bit lonely for human company. Still, he always told himself, things could be worse. He had Smudge's company, and other animals to talk to. And so, most of the time, he and Smudge lived quite peacefully in the little cottage by the roadside.

Or at least they had been able to live peacefully, before the terrible heatwave had settled over the land, threatening to ruin everything.

The heatwave had begun in early spring. At the time everyone had been delighted with the fine weather so early in the year. But they stopped being delighted when the heatwave went on and on, as if it would never end.

The sun stayed blazingly hot, all day and every day. The sky stayed amazingly clear, all day and all night, with never a wisp of cloud to be seen. Which meant, of course, never a drop of rain.

As the heatwave went on, week after week, month after month, it caused a frightening drought. Slowly, steadily, the land began to dry up. Rivers shrank to the size of brooks, while brooks disappeared entirely. All the trees and other plants faded and wilted, their leaves turning brown and dead. All the animals weakened and drooped, suffering with thirst.

And everywhere in the land, the people suffered too. From thirst, as their wells and streams dried up. From hunger, as their gardens and crops withered. And from fear, as the heat and drought went on, and the land grew ever more sun-scorched and waterless.

Malcolm suffered a little less than others,

because when any plants died in his garden he used his magic to grow more. But the plants that he grew magically were still ordinary plants, needing water to go on growing and stay alive. And he didn't have any magic that could find water or that could make it rain.

So he was just as worried and fearful as everyone else, while the heatwave went endlessly on, and the land grew drier and drier.

He was certainly worried that morning, when he went out – with Smudge on his shoulder – to look at his garden. As well as the dead tomato plants, a great many lettuces and cabbages and other vegetables had grown brown and wilted, as had most of his patch of corn. Also, his hens weren't pecking busily around, but were sitting limply in the shade, looking very unhappy. And his cow was drooping miserably under a tree on the far side of the garden.

As usual, Malcolm went to his well to draw up some water for the cow and the hens. But when the bucket came up, it was less than half-full of water, which looked brownish and slightly scummy.

"Coo!" Smudge said, peering into the bucket. "That's nasty!"

Malcolm peered down into the well, sighing as he saw how low the water level was. "If it doesn't rain soon," he said, "we'll be in trouble."

"Everybody will," Smudge agreed gloomily.

But the sky was as cloudless as ever, its normal blue faded almost to white by the sun's glare. And the air was as thick and heavy with heat as it had been through all the months of the drought. So while Malcolm poured the water into the small trough where the cow and the hens could get to it, he was almost too worried to chat to them as he usually did. At the same time, he suddenly felt very weary, and was unable to hold back one huge yawn and then another.

Smudge put his head on one side and gave

him a knowing look. "You tired, Malc?" he asked. "Didn't sleep well last night?"

"Probably not," Malcolm said vaguely.

Smudge bobbed his head several times, disapprovingly. "You went out, right? Prob'ly round to that Alice's. Doin' more secret magic, growin' things in 'er garden..."

Malcolm looked a bit embarrassed. Alice was the pretty daughter of a neighbouring farmer, and Malcolm had liked her a lot for a long time. He also had the idea that she might like him, but he could never be sure, because he was hardly ever able to speak to her. Alice's father was one of the people who thought that Malcolm was either a fool or a lunatic, if not both, and so he tried to keep his daughter away from Malcolm as much as he could.

Even so, during the heatwave Malcolm had often gone out after dark to creep secretly into Alice's garden, where he had used his magic to grow vegetables for her and, sometimes, flowers.

"Her father's crop's almost completely ruined," Malcolm explained to Smudge. "I couldn't bear it if she didn't have enough to eat."

"Yer mad, you are," Smudge said, flicking his tail sharply. "You can't feed 'er an' 'er family all by yerself. You know 'ow doin' a lot of magic wears you out."

"That doesn't matter," Malcolm said. "I can't let her go hungry, if the drought leaves them with nothing."

"Wot if they find out it's you growin' that stuff?" Smudge demanded.

"That wouldn't matter much either," Malcolm said.

"Oh, yes, it would," Smudge told him. "Use yer 'ead, can't you? *Everybody's* crop is dyin' in the drought. *Everybody's* gonna be goin' 'ungry, if it keeps on. An' if they find out you got magic that can grow food, you could 'ave everybody from the village an' all round 'ere bangin' on yer door, wantin' you to give 'em somethin' to eat!"

Malcolm looked shocked. "I hadn't thought of that..."

"You didn't think at all," Smudge said. "I know you – if that did 'appen you'd prob'ly try yer best to feed 'em all, an' you'd wear yerself out an' ruin yer 'ealth doin' that much magic. An' wot if the word got out, maybe to the city? Malc, you could 'ave 'undreds an' *thousands* of 'ungry folk at the door! An' tryin' to feed them wouldn't just wear you out – it could finish you off!"

Malcolm looked even more upset. "I suppose you're right..."

"'Course I am," Smudge said. "Look out for yerself, that's wot I say, an' let other folk look out for themselves. *You* can't stop the drought an' save the land, Malc. All you can do is keep yerself goin', an' 'ope we get some rain before everythin' dies."

Chapter 2

The Hawk's Story

Malcolm sighed unhappily. He couldn't disagree with Smudge. It was true that he couldn't stop the drought, and that he wouldn't be able to feed huge crowds of starving people, if it came to that. But at the same time, he thought, Smudge's advice – about just looking out for himself – seemed so … so *selfish*. And, he thought stubbornly, he still meant what he had said before. No matter what, he wouldn't let Alice go hungry.

Wearily, he put the bucket away and went to deal with his tomatoes. First he peeled the dry brown tendrils away from the sticks that supported them and pulled up the dead plants. Then he took a deep breath and frowned as he stared intently down at the soil.

Immediately small delicate shoots began to pop up, bright green against the ground's dry greyness.

Swiftly the shoots grew bigger. They stretched up, sprouted leaves, wrapped coiling tendrils around the supporting sticks. Small flowers appeared among the leaves, quickly turning into little green spheres that began to swell and change colour. Within a few more seconds, each of the new plants held several big, red, ripe tomatoes.

And then Malcolm jumped with sudden surprise, for a sharp voice spoke almost directly above his head.

"That's a good trick," the voice said.

As Malcolm looked up, shading his eyes against the sky's brightness, Smudge shrank back on his shoulder with a nervous mutter.

A large bird with rusty-brown feathers, fierce eyes and a hooked beak was sitting in the tree at the edge of the garden. Some kind of hawk, Malcolm thought, stroking Smudge's feathers soothingly.

"Morning," he said to the hawk calmly.

The hawk flared his wings, startled. "That's another good trick," it said in its harsh voice, "talking to birds. You must be a magician."

"Not much of one," Malcolm said. "You've seen the only two kinds of magic I can do."

"It must be interesting, though," the hawk said, "talking to all the birds. And it would be useful, if you like eating plants." It peered at Malcolm hopefully. "Could you magic up some *meat* for me?"

"Sorry, no," Malcolm said. "But I've got some bacon in the house that you could have."

He went back to the cottage with Smudge to find the bacon, and took it back out to the tree, where the hawk devoured it in two gulps.

"That was nice," the hawk said. It eyed

Smudge. "Some fresh pigeon might be even nicer."

"Wot's 'e sayin'?" Smudge asked, shrinking again under the fierce yellow gaze.

"Smudge is my friend," Malcolm told the hawk firmly. "I'll want you to remember that, if you're staying around here."

"If you say so," the hawk replied disappointedly. "But you don't have to worry. I'm just passing through."

"Where are you going?" Malcolm asked.

"North," the hawk said. "I've heard that there's good wild country up there, and I want to get as far north as I can."

"Really?" Malcolm said, interested. "Why?"

The hawk snapped its beak. "I used to live a long way south of here, in a place called the Hidden Valley. It was lovely there – no humans anywhere, lots of nesting places, plenty to eat. But it's been ruined by all this heat and drought. It's nothing but bare dry sand there now, just an empty desert."

"That's terrible!" Malcolm said.

"That's not all," the hawk went on fiercely. "Since the drought has gone on and on, the desert has been *growing.* All around the edges of the Hidden Valley, the plants have been dying and the earth has been drying up and turning to dusty sand. Every day, for months, the desert has grown a little bigger, spreading a little farther. If this heat keeps up, without any rain, that desert in the south could spread over the whole country. In a few more months, there might not be anything left, anywhere, but dead empty sand."

"But that isn't likely," Malcolm said worriedly. "Surely it's going to rain some time soon. It *has* to!"

"No, it doesn't," the hawk said harshly. "It won't ever rain again unless someone does something about the giant."

"What giant?" Malcolm asked, startled.

"Don't you know about the giant?" asked the hawk. "He's a great huge monster, man-shaped but much, much bigger. He showed up in the Hidden Valley back in the early spring, no one knows where from. He made himself a big high tower out of a strange kind of stone, and then he just … took over. He's ugly and cruel and nasty, and he has some kind of *magical* thing that makes him even stronger. He's the worst thing the Valley has ever known."

"I've never heard anything about a giant," Malcolm said doubtfully.

"I suppose you wouldn't," the hawk said. "There haven't been any people in the Hidden Valley for ages, so news of him wouldn't have got out. But the birds and the animals know all about him, I can tell you. That's why so many of us have left the Valley."

Malcolm frowned, puzzled. "I thought you left because of the drought, because the Valley has become a desert. What has this giant got to do with that?"

"He started it," the hawk said simply.

"Started what?" Malcolm asked. "What do you mean?"

"He started the whole thing," the hawk replied. "The heatwave, the drought, all of it. He used his magical power to steal the *clouds* out of the sky. Then he locked them away in his tower, so that it would never rain again."

For a long moment Malcolm stared at the hawk in silence, his eyes wide and his mouth open. It was the most astonishing story he had ever heard – that the heat and drought weren't natural, but were caused by an evil giant who had stolen all the clouds from the sky.

"Is that … really true?" Malcolm asked at last.

The hawk glared at him. "Hawks don't lie. And you'll probably get other birds from the Hidden Valley coming this way, so ask them if you don't believe me."

"Oh, I believe you," Malcolm said quickly. "It's just … hard to take in, all at once. And I can't understand *why* the giant would want to steal the clouds and start the drought."

"He likes heat and dryness, I expect," the hawk said. "Most of all, he seems to like hot dry *sand,* where nothing can grow. Some of the other birds said that he even made his tower out of sand, using his magic. I think he likes sand so much that he stole the clouds to make the Hidden Valley into a desert, and to start the desert spreading everywhere."

"But everything will die!" Malcolm cried.

"That's right," the hawk said harshly, "unless something can be done about the giant. I suppose it would take a very powerful magician to stop him – but if he isn't stopped, this whole country could become nothing but dead, dry, empty sand."

And with that he rose from the branch and soared into the cloudless sky, heading north.

"Coo!" Smudge muttered when Malcolm told him what the hawk had been saying.

"Maybe we should start thinkin' about goin' north too."

Malcolm was frowning thoughtfully. "No," he said. "The drought and the desert would catch up with us there after a while. I think, instead, I should go to the city."

"What for?" Smudge asked with amazement.

"To tell someone," Malcolm said firmly. "Probably no one else knows about the giant, if they haven't been talking to birds from the Hidden Valley. We have to tell the government or someone."

"From wot that 'awk said about the giant," Smudge remarked, "you'd do better tellin' some bigwig magicians."

"Right!" Malcolm said. "That's what I'll do. I'll go and see the head of the Wizard School in the city, and tell him."

"D'you reckon 'e'll listen to you?" Smudge asked. "Wasn't 'e the one wouldn't let you into 'is School?"

"I'll make him listen," Malcolm said with determination. "He has to know the truth about the drought."

"You could just get yerself into trouble," Smudge warned.

Malcolm shrugged. "I have to try, Smudge. Something has to be done to stop the giant."

"If 'e *can* be stopped," Smudge muttered. "I just 'ope we don't 'ave a long 'ot trip to the city for nothin'."

"You don't have to come, Smudge, if you'd rather not," Malcolm said.

Smudge peered up at the sky. "I ain't stayin' 'ere by myself," he announced. "Not with bloomin' '*awks* flyin' around."

Chapter 3

Wizard School

They set off at once along the road that would take them to the village, and from there, on a bigger highway, to the city. Malcolm trudged along in silence, weighed down by his thoughts and the heat, and keeping his mouth closed against the dust-cloud raised by his feet. Once or twice Smudge took to the air, to escape the dust and make a bit of a breeze, but he usually came back soon to Malcolm's shoulder, also saying very little as they went on.

Their mood improved somewhat when they

reached the village, where they had a drink from the well on the village green and rested briefly in the shade. Then Malcolm brightened even more. He saw Alice shopping in the village, without her father, and went to speak to her.

Alice seemed just as pleased to see him, but soon her smile changed to a worried frown when he told her that he was going to the city, to the Wizard School, with an important message. He didn't tell her what the message was, because he didn't want to upset her. But she seemed upset enough as it was.

"Malcolm, I don't understand," Alice said. "Why should *you* be taking a message to the Wizard School?"

"Um..." Malcolm said. He had kept his own small magics a secret even from Alice, and right then didn't seem the best time to tell her. "I can't really talk about the message just now, Alice. Sorry. But ... I'll probably be able to tell you all about it fairly soon."

Alice was still frowning worriedly, but she nodded. "All right. Will you be away for long?"

"I don't know," Malcolm said. "I hope not."

She nodded again. "If you like, I could try to go over now and then to look after your cow and chickens."

"That would be really kind," Malcolm said gratefully. "And … um … maybe you could come over some time when I get back, as well."

"I'll try," she said.

After that, Malcolm whistled happily most of the way to the city, despite the dust of the bigger highway and some teasing from Smudge. Then Smudge suggested that Malcolm might become a hero for discovering the cause of the drought, causing Alice's father to feel more friendly towards him. And that idea was making Malcolm whistle even more happily as they reached the city.

The outskirts of the city looked, at first, much like the village where they had been earlier, with the same small wooden buildings and bare streets. But there were a great many *more* buildings and streets, and the difference was even greater as they went closer to the city centre. The buildings there were much bigger, and were often made of stone. And the streets were wider as well, crowded with wagons and carts and carriages, with paths alongside for people to walk on, and with cobbles or paving-stones instead of bare earth.

Malcolm gazed around with interest, even though he had been to the city before. But Smudge was scowling with disapproval. He had been born and raised in the city, but since he had wandered away and met Malcolm, he no longer cared for city ways.

"There's more bloomin' pigeons than ever," he grumbled. "Too many, if you ask me – scruffy beggars… An' too many people an' all. Give me a nice bit of countryside any time."

"We won't be staying long," Malcolm told him. "Look, at the end of that street. That's the Wizard School."

The School was an enormous building made of bright stone, with a lot of tall towers as if it was trying to look like a castle, standing apart from other buildings. It also looked quiet and empty, which made Malcolm guess that it might be summer holidays for the students.

But the big main door opened readily enough, and Malcolm stepped in, peering with some nervousness along the empty corridor that stretched before him. He could remember the way, from his first visit, but at that moment the idea of marching into the office of the head of the Wizard School was making his knees feel a little shaky.

And when he and Smudge reached the office of the head of the School, he felt even more nervous. Because there seemed to be very little chance of anyone marching in. The door of the office had a sign on it: "CEDRIC COLCOZZEN, LORD HIGH WIZARD". In front of the door, as if to guard it, was a tall narrow table at which sat a tall narrow woman with a long sharp nose and a thin mouth that did not seem ever to have smiled.

The woman had a smaller sign on her table, which read: "Miss Peck, Secretary". And she sniffed at Malcolm with disapproval as he explained that he had come with an important message for the High Wizard.

"You cannot possibly see the High Wizard," sniffed Miss Peck. "He is much too busy."

"Then I'll wait," Malcolm said, and he went to sit on a narrow wooden chair against the wall.

"What are you doing with that bird?" Miss Peck demanded. "I won't have birds in here."

Malcolm was beginning to feel more annoyed than nervous. "Smudge," he said quietly, "fly around a bit, with a lot of flapping and swooping down and things."

Smudge chuckled. "'Avin' a bit of fun, are we?"

He flew up from Malcolm's shoulder,

circling the room with a lot of noisy wild flapping like a frantic bird trying to escape. With every circle, he also swooped down near Miss Peck, making her squawk and duck and clutch at her tightly pinned hair.

"Stop it!" she shrieked. "Get it out of here!"

"He just needs a place to sit while we wait," Malcolm said, trying to keep from laughing. "I'll make him one."

He stared hard at the centre of her table. At once, from the polished wood, a green shoot appeared, uncurling and stretching up as it grew. A moment later, there was a small graceful tree growing out of the table, its branches tipped with feathery leaves. Miss Peck jerked back as Smudge fluttered down to perch calmly in the little tree.

"You didn't say you were magical," Miss Peck said, glaring at Malcolm.

"That's not why I'm here," Malcolm said. "I told you, I have an important message for the High Wizard – about the drought. And my bird and I are going to get very restless if we have to wait too long."

Miss Peck's tight mouth went even tighter. Without a word, she got up and marched through the door into the High Wizard's office. A moment later, she came out and beckoned sharply to Malcolm, holding the door open.

Suddenly dry-mouthed as his nervousness returned, Malcolm put Smudge on his shoulder and went through into the presence of the High Wizard.

The wizard's office was broad and impressive, with rich rugs on the floor and elegant drapes around the tall windows. The wizard himself, Cedric Colcozzen, sat at a huge desk carved from dark, shiny stone. He wore a long blue-green robe made of some costly material, and though his hair and beard were grey, his eyebrows were thick and dark, and were drawn down in a scowl as he stared at Malcolm. In one hand he held a slender staff, bright with jewels, which he tapped impatiently against the side of his desk.

"Why have you been upsetting Miss Peck?" Colcozzen demanded as Malcolm approached.

"I..." Malcolm clutched at his courage and his voice. "I had to see you, sir. I've ... found out what's causing the drought."

The High Wizard raised his black eyebrows. "You have burst into my office to talk about the *weather*?"

"No, sir," Malcolm gulped. "It's ... I was told by a hawk..."

He jumped as Colcozzen smacked the end of his jewelled staff on to the floor. "Birds!" the wizard snapped. "Yes, now I remember! I *know* you, don't I? Morton or something..."

"Malcolm," said Malcolm.

"Indeed," Colcozzen went on. "You applied for a place here once. You can talk to birds and beasts, and grow plants, but nothing else. Correct?"

"Yes," Malcolm said glumly.

The wizard nodded. "And I decided it would be pointless for you to study here, with such small common-or-*garden* powers." He made a strange wheezing sound, and Malcolm realized that he was laughing at his own joke. But the laughter vanished as he scowled again. "I hope you're not trying to wheedle your way into the School with this tale about a hawk."

"No," Malcolm said firmly, some of his annoyance returning. "The hawk simply told me about the drought." And before Colcozzen could interrupt, he told the story as the hawk had told him, about the giant with the evil magic, the stolen clouds and the spreading desert. As he spoke, the High Wizard's scowl grew steadily darker.

"What utter nonsense!" Colcozzen said at last. "Are you trying to play some foolish trick? Don't you know that giants are never magical? The Little People, yes, of course – elves, gnomes, goblins – they all have their own magic. But there has never been a magical *giant* in the history of the world!"

"I didn't know that," Malcolm said.

Colcozzen sneered. "I think you're either a fool or a rogue, and I've wasted enough time on you."

"But wouldn't a magical *thing* still work," Malcolm said desperately, "whoever had it? A charm or a wand ... or something like your staff?"

The wizard tightened his grip on the staff, scowling. "I suppose that's so," he said. "Anyone could use a magical object."

"And there *is* something odd about the drought," Malcolm went on. "Or else surely you and the other wizards would have been able to make it rain, magically."

Colcozzen snorted. "Many wizards, including myself, have tried to end the drought. But not even the greatest of wizards can make rain when there are no clouds to work with..."

He stopped, suddenly realizing what he had said.

"Maybe there aren't any clouds because someone has stolen them," Malcolm said pointedly. "Someone like a giant with a magical object, who likes dry sand and deserts."

Colcozzen frowned again. "It still sounds ridiculous..."

"But what if it's true?" Malcolm asked. "Couldn't you at least look into it? That shouldn't take long, for a High Wizard."

"Of course not," Colcozzen said with a sniff.

"And if the story is true," Malcolm added, "and *you* were the one to defeat the giant and end the drought, single-handed..."

"Ye-es," Colcozzen said thoughtfully, his eyes glinting with the prospect of glory. "That might be very worthwhile. Yes, I expect it is my duty to investigate this wild tale. I shall visit this Hidden Valley, at magical speed, and see what is to be seen." He got to his feet, looking down his nose at Malcolm. "And if your story turns out to be a fool's fancy or a trickster's lie, I shall return at the same speed, and make you regret it!"

He stalked to the door, then turned. "I think you can wait here for my return," he told Malcolm. "If this does turn out to be a waste of time, I shall want to know where to find you."

He opened the door, stepped through and closed it again firmly. "Miss Peck," Malcolm heard him say from the door's other side, "I am going out, for no more than an hour. Please make sure that the young man remains in my office till I return."

And with that Malcolm heard the sound of a heavy key being turned in the lock.

Chapter 4

Getting Away

"'Ere!" Smudge said angrily. "'E can't just keep us 'ere, like prisoners!"

Malcolm shook his head. "I think he can. A High Wizard can do just as he likes, most of the time. But it doesn't matter. He said he'll only be an hour, travelling by magic. And if he finds that the hawk's story is true, there won't be a problem."

"I still don't like bein' locked up," Smudge fumed. He took to the air, swooping around the office, settling at last on a window sill. Even with the heat of the day the windows were closed – and seemed to be locked,

Malcolm saw, in some way that was probably magical.

Smudge was watching a wasp that was buzzing against the window, looking hopelessly for a way out. "I know 'ow 'e feels," he said. "Maybe we could smash the glass."

"I don't think we should cause any damage," Malcolm said. "Come on – we just have to wait for the wizard to get back."

They settled themselves on a lush sofa, and began to wait. It was very boring, since there wasn't much to look at or to do, and nothing to read except some old books about magic that Malcolm didn't understand. Smudge kept asking, " 'ow long now?" every five minutes or so, until Malcolm made him stop. But after quite a long while, the wait began to be a little worrying as well as boring.

"It must be long past an hour now," Malcolm said at last, getting up and going to the door. "Miss Peck?" he called. "Shouldn't the High Wizard be back by now?"

"He'll be back when he chooses to be back," Miss Peck replied, her voice still sounding sniffy although it was muffled by the door.

Sighing, Malcolm went back to the sofa. But Smudge flew over to the window sill again, to look outside, while keeping an eye on the wasp still buzzing against the glass. And they waited and waited, while time crawled by as if it had taken lessons from a snail.

After another long time, Malcolm was even more worried. He was sure that the wizard wouldn't have forgotten about him, after all his threats. Now he began to wonder, a bit fearfully, whether Colcozzen hadn't come back because he *couldn't*. Perhaps the evil giant had been too much for him...

He went to the door again. "Miss Peck!" he called. "The High Wizard doesn't seem to be coming back, and I want to get out of here!"

He thought he heard a sniff from beyond the door, but no other reply.

"Maybe she's cleared off," Smudge said.

"I hope not," Malcolm said, annoyed. "We could be here all night." He thumped on the door. "Miss Peck!" he shouted.

Still no reply. And when he stooped to look through the keyhole, he could see nothing because the big brass key had been left in the lock on the other side. That gave Malcolm an idea. If he could poke the key out of the lock so that it fell on the floor, he might be able to reach under the door with something thin and pull the key through to his side.

He looked around the office, and spotted a long, slim poker hanging beside the empty fireplace. Just the thing, he thought. First, though, he had to know whether Miss Peck was still at her desk, because she might grab the key and stop him. And to find out where she was, he would need some help.

With Smudge on his shoulder, he went over to the wasp that was still buzzing tirelessly against the window. "Excuse me," he said politely.

The wasp swooped down to hover directly in front of his face. As Malcolm knew, wasps are hardly ever afraid of anything, and nearly always angry about something. And this one seemed no different.

"What?" the wasp demanded in its small buzzy voice. "What?"

"I wonder if you'd do something for me," Malcolm said.

"What?" the wasp buzzed again. "Why should I?"

"Because we're all prisoners here," Malcolm replied calmly. "But if you help me to get out of this room, where the windows are all locked by magic, I'll let you out of a window in another room."

The wasp flew in a small circle, then hovered again. "If this is a trick," it said, "I'll sting you and your bird too."

"It's no trick," Malcolm said. "I just need you to crawl under the door and see if there's a woman sitting in the other room."

"Why?" the wasp demanded.

"Because if she's there," Malcolm replied, "we'll have to wait for her to go away before we can get out."

The wasp buzzed away, making a complete circuit of the room while it made up its mind. At last it swooped down on to the floor and crawled out through the narrow space under the door. Hurrying to the door, Malcolm and Smudge faintly heard the wasp buzzing. Then they heard a gasp, some thrashing noises, a shriek, and finally the sound of running foot-steps.

The wasp crawled back under the door, then flew up to face Malcolm again. "There was a woman there," it said, sounding pleased with itself. "So I stung her, and she ran away. Now let me out."

"Um..." Malcolm said, feeling a little sorry for Miss Peck. "Right. I just have to get the key."

He used the poker to push the big key out

of the keyhole, then he slid the poker under the door and after some scrabbling around finally managed to drag the key through to him. A moment later they were in the outer room, where there was no sign of Miss Peck. Malcolm opened a window and the wasp flew away without a word.

"Charmin'," Smudge remarked.

"Never mind," Malcolm said. "We're out. Now let's get away from here."

They left the Wizard School without seeing anyone, and were soon hurrying out of the city on the big highway that would take them home. The heat and the dust kept Malcolm silent as before, but so did feelings of worry and gloom. He felt that he had failed, after having set off so full of hope that something might be done about the drought. He also feared something dreadful might have happened to the High Wizard.

"Are we just leavin' it, then?" Smudge asked, breaking the silence.

Malcolm shrugged unhappily. “I don’t know what else to do.”

“Ain’t there anyone else you could tell?” Smudge asked.

Malcolm looked even unhappier. “I don’t want to go back to the Wizard School and tell the other wizards. They might just lock us up again and wait for Colcozzen.”

“I ain’t ’avin’ that,” Smudge said.

“All we can do is go home,” Malcolm said. “Maybe there’s a reason why Colcozzen was delayed. Maybe he’s dealing with the giant right now.”

But they both went on feeling worried and gloomy the rest of the way to the village, and then along the smaller road to the cottage. By then they were also quite tired, for it had been a long and eventful day, and dusk was gathering.

At home, Malcolm saw that his cow and his hens were quite all right, which made him think of Alice, which made him feel a little better. After a quick supper Smudge flew up to his roost on a rafter and Malcolm went to bed too.

He slept poorly, with vague dreams about an empty, deathly desert where the sun was only centimetres above his head. And in the morning he dragged himself through his chores, still feeling worried and gloomy and tired, and even more upset by the low level of the water in his well.

His spirits lifted briefly when Alice arrived unexpectedly to see if he had come home. But it was not a successful visit. She was still curious about his trip to the city and his secret message, and she had become more curious, because of some troubling news from the village.

"Someone came from the city today," she told Malcolm, "and said that the High Wizard of the Wizard School had *disappeared*! And the constables are looking for a stranger who visited him yesterday! And you said you were going there, Malcolm – do you know anything about it?"

"Um..." Malcolm said unhappily. "Not really."

"What was it all about, then?" Alice asked with a frown. "Did you see the High Wizard yesterday?"

Malcolm felt trapped. He wanted to tell her, just to stop her looking at him that way, but he knew he couldn't. Miss Peck had probably told the constables all about him and his magical escape from the School. The constables, and perhaps some other wizards, might be looking for him right then, and might be thinking he was somehow to blame for the High Wizard's disappearance.

If he told Alice about it, she would probably tell her father, who might tell others, and so the news would spread. Then the constables would know just where to find him.

In the end he just shook his head. "I'll tell you some time, Alice," he said wanly, "but not now."

She got to her feet, annoyed. "Sometimes, Malcolm, I wonder if my father and everyone might be right when they talk about how – how *weird* you are! *Keep* your silly secrets, then! I just hope you haven't got yourself into some kind of trouble!"

And she flounced angrily out of the door and away.

"Coo!" Smudge said from his roost on the rafter. "Wot's got 'er so 'uffy?"

"Me," Malcolm said sadly, "because I wouldn't tell her what I've been doing. And Colcozzen has disappeared, so I suppose she's suspicious."

" 'Oo wouldn't be?" Smudge said. "But never mind, Malc. If the wizard does beat the giant some'ow, an' ends the drought, you'll be an 'ero an' she'll be 'appy with you again."

"But what if the giant has beaten the wizard?" Malcolm asked.

"Then the drought'll get worse," Smudge

said, “an’ you’ll ’ave more to worry about than ’er.”

“That’s right,” Malcolm said, going to the door and staring gloomily out. “I just wish we knew what was happening. I wish another bird would come along and tell us what’s going on in that Hidden Valley, and where Colcozzen is.”

“If that ’awk was still around,” Smudge said, “you could ask ’im to go ’ave a look.”

Malcolm turned, looking at Smudge with a strange look in his eyes. “I don’t think I need the hawk.”

“Don’t look at me!” Smudge said, flaring his wings nervously. “I ain’t a carrier pigeon!”

“No,” Malcolm said, the strange look in his eyes growing stronger. “I was thinking more of … going to the Valley myself.”

Chapter 5
Southward Bound

"You must be off yer 'ead!" Smudge cried, his feathers seeming to stand on end with shock. "Go there yerself? 'As the 'eat cooked yer brain?"

"I just want to know what's going on," Malcolm said stubbornly.

"A nasty giant is turnin' the land into a desert!" Smudge said. "An' the 'Igh Wizard's disappeared! *That's* wot's goin' on! D'you want to disappear too? Or d'you reckon you can fight the giant yerself?"

"Of course not," Malcolm said. "But I have to do *something.* No one knows about the giant but us – and Colcozzen, wherever he is. And I daren't go and tell anyone else. Not with constables looking for me and everything. So it's sort of up to me, in a way. Just to go and look, at least – and maybe find out just what has happened to the High Wizard, in case the constables come."

Smudge fluttered his tail. "I s'pose it makes some sense. At least we'd be somewhere else if constables come lookin'. But the Valley … I dunno, Malc."

"I'd have to be careful, I know," Malcolm said. "But some of the creatures who live there might help to spy out the land for me. And I can always grow things to eat, even in a desert. I'd be fine, Smudge, really. And I wouldn't stay long. Just long enough to see what's going on."

Smudge peered at him dubiously. "You sure you ain't thinkin' of doin' somethin' silly, tryin' to be an 'ero, so Alice an' everybody'll like you better?"

Malcolm sighed. "No, Smudge. I wish there *was* something I could do. But I know I'm not a hero. Nor a wizard, either."

Smudge bobbed his head firmly. "That's all right, Malc. You don't want to go takin' chances, wearin' yerself out, tryin' to save the world single-'anded. We'll just take a quick look around the Valley, an' then 'op it."

"We?" Malcolm echoed, with a small smile.

"You ain't goin' alone," Smudge told him firmly. "*Somebody* with some sense 'as to go along an' look after you."

Once the decision had been made, they took very little time to get ready for the journey. Malcolm put some clothes in a small backpack, along with part of a loaf of bread for Smudge, and that was their packing done. Then he spent a while writing a note to Alice, tearing it up and starting again, over and over. In the end it was a very vague note, apologizing for upsetting her, saying that he had to go away again for a while but would explain everything when he got back, and asking her to put some water out for his cow and hens, if she wouldn't mind.

"If there's any water in the well to *be* put out," he said gloomily to Smudge.

For the rest of that day they did very little, and then went to bed early. So they were up and having a bite of breakfast before sunrise. And as the sun's blaze rose into the cloudless sky Malcolm looked around, sighed, wondered if he was being dangerously foolish, and then finally set off with Smudge on his shoulder, heading south.

He wondered several more times, in the first few hours, if he was being foolish. Certainly there was nothing enjoyable about the journey, even in those early stages. The narrow back road was so completely empty, as were the sun-dried fields on either side, that Malcolm began to feel as if he and Smudge were the only things left alive on the ruined landscape. And even when they did finally see other creatures – a horse slumped under a dying tree, a faraway bird like a moving scar on the white-hot sky – it didn't improve the mood.

Nor did the road itself, which was often little better than a blurred track. With every step the powdery dust rose in a cloud, settling on Malcolm's clothes, stinging his eyes and gathering grittily in his mouth and throat, so he and Smudge stopped quite often, to rest and let the dust settle and to have a drink provided by Malcolm's magic.

Usually he would grow a small plant beside the road – a bush or vine bearing the juicier sort of fruit such as melons or oranges. That provided food as well as drink, though Smudge also had the bit of bread to peck at. They seldom ate much, for the crushing heat seemed to dry up their appetites along with everything else. And the fruit-bearing bush or vine would start to wither and die within minutes on the waterless soil, as if to show once again how desperate and fearful the drought had become.

Travelling was no more pleasant after the sun's fury had set. The night was almost as hot and just as dusty as the day, and brought with it small flying, biting insects that paid no attention when Malcolm asked them nicely to go away. They slept badly on the first night, under the thin branches of a hedge by the road, and in a nightmare Malcolm saw himself unable to move as a towering ridge of desert sand swept towards him like a tidal wave and buried him.

The dream stayed in Malcolm's mind throughout the next day as he and Smudge went on their way, still wrapped in their private dust cloud. But they slept a little better on the second night, when some friendly field mice showed Malcolm a haystack that made a fairly comfortable bed. In return, Malcolm grew a berry bush for the mice, as well as more fruit for Smudge and himself.

Then, on the third day, the narrow back road brought them to a far wider and much more important highway, which was the main route to the southern part of the land.

"Coo!" Smudge said when they first saw the big main road. "Look at 'em all! Wot a mob!"

Malcolm was astonished. The big road seemed to be full of people – on their own, in couples or families, in bigger groups that might have been several families together. They were in wagons or carts, on horses or donkeys, or straggling along on foot – all choking and gasping in the storms of dust stirred up by their feet and hooves and wheels.

And they were all going in the same direction. North.

Out on the big road, where he was the only one travelling south, Malcolm nodded in a friendly fashion at the people he passed, but he soon stopped, because not one of them ever returned his nod, and most didn't even look at him. They all seemed completely wrapped up in their own misery, overcome by heat and thirst, coughing in the dust, bent and sagging with weariness.

Malcolm felt desperately sorry for them. It was clear that they were travelling north because they had been driven out of their southern homes by the drought – and perhaps by the spread of the deadly desert out of the Hidden Valley. And that made Malcolm even more nervous about his own journey.

"I wonder if it's already too late," he said to Smudge, after watching more groups of homeless people trudge past. "Even if the drought can be stopped, the land might be ruined for ever, especially in the south."

"Maybe not," Smudge said. "Not if some rain falls, some'ow, before long."

"Then we'll have to find someone who can

make that happen," Malcolm said determinedly, "once we tell them what we find in the Valley."

"If we get back in one piece to tell 'em," Smudge muttered.

That dire thought silenced Malcolm again as he plodded on, one lone figure southward-bound among the endless stream of people going north.

After a time, they passed a group of people who were unlike most of the other travellers. They were five big, rough-looking men who weren't carrying loads of belongings like the others. And, unusually, they not only looked at Malcolm as he passed, but stopped and stared at him – in a cold, ugly way, as if sizing him up.

"Don't like the look of that lot," Smudge said as they went past. "Wot they lookin' at, anyway?"

"I don't know," Malcolm said uneasily, increasing his pace.

"'Ere!" Smudge said, turning to peer back at the five men. "They ain't just lookin', Malc! They're *followin'* us!"

His stomach tightening with alarm, Malcolm walked even faster. He tried to tell himself that the men might simply have changed their minds about going north, but he knew that was unlikely. It was more probable that they were robbers or something, who saw him as an easy victim.

And, to make things worse, his shadow was getting longer as the day moved towards evening.

By the time darkness was settling on the land, Malcolm decided to get off the road and try to hide from the five men still following along behind him. Ahead, he saw a stand of trees close to the roadside – most of them half-dead, but with thickets of dry brush in among them, dense and shadowy. He crept in among those shadows, huddling with Smudge at the foot of a tree.

As the darkness deepened, an eerie silence fell. The other travellers on the road had also found places to spend the night, so the road was quiet, and there seemed also to be no creatures moving within the woods. Before long, Malcolm began to relax, and Smudge went to sleep.

When a bright half-moon rose later to push back the shadows, Malcolm decided to have something to eat before his empty stomach's rumbling got any louder. Creeping away carefully so as not to waken Smudge, he found a small open clearing covered in tall dry grass and weeds, and there he used his magic to grow a nice watermelon that would take care of his hunger and thirst all at once.

He had just cut himself a juicy piece when the five big shadowy figures stepped silently out of the woods into the clearing.

With a cry, Malcolm dropped the watermelon and scrambled to his feet. It was the five men who had followed him on the road, and they were looking at him with cruel smiles.

"That was *magic,* that was!" one of them said. "Just grew himself his dinner!"

"We're in luck, lads," said the biggest and roughest-looking of the five. "We won't rob this one. We'll tie him up and take him with us – and make him magic up food for us whenever we want!"

Chapter 6

Across the Plain

For a moment the terrible threat made Malcolm's mind go blank and his body go rigid with shock. But then Smudge, roosting on a low branch nearby, stirred at the sound of voices.

"Wossat?" he said sleepily.

It was just what Malcolm needed to bring him back to himself, and make his mind start working again. "Smudge," he said, "wake up – and fly off into the trees where you'll be safe."

He had of course spoken in pigeon language, which sounded like a strange bubbling to other humans. The five men laughed cruelly. "He's so scared he can't talk," said one of them.

"He don't need to talk," growled the biggest one, who was clearly the leader. "He just needs to start magickin' us some dinner."

Still looking frightened, Malcolm had lowered his head slightly, and now stared intently at the grass around the men's feet. Then they all jumped as Smudge suddenly flapped up from the low branch, away among the shadowed trees, and while the men's attention was caught by Smudge, Malcolm whirled and bolted into the woods.

At once, yelling, the men started after him. But they hadn't noticed that while Malcolm had been looking at the ground, he had been growing a low tangle of briars around their feet. As they charged forward after him, their feet caught in the snarls of the briars, and all five of them crashed heavily to the ground.

It was all the headstart that Malcolm needed. By the time the furious men had regained their feet, he was deep in the woods, out of sight in the darkness. And by the time they managed to stop shouting and cursing and thought about listening, Malcolm was tucked into a hollow among the roots of a big tree, still and silent.

"He's hidin' somewhere," he heard the big leader growl in his rough voice. "Spread out and look for him."

Malcolm shrank down into the hollow, listening to the occasional snap and crackle of dry twigs as the men searched through the woods. As the moon was so bright, he quickly grew some short bristly thorn bushes to form an almost solid barrier around himself. He had just finished when he heard footsteps approaching.

"Look at them thorns," he heard one of the men say.

"Yeah – he won't have gone in there," said

another. "Let's go."

They moved away, their sounds fading as they went farther into the woods. Malcolm sighed with relief, sinking back into the hollow, hoping that Smudge had also found a good spot up in the trees. And before long, because he was tired after the long day and the scary night, he fell asleep.

The next thing he knew, Smudge landed on his chest to waken him and to announce that the sun was rising and there was no sign of the robbers anywhere in the area. "Good trick with the thorn bushes, Malc," Smudge said, staring around. "Just one thing, though. 'Ow you gonna get out?"

Malcolm gazed around, taken aback. He hadn't thought of that problem. While he could grow plants, he couldn't *un*-grow them. But in the end he managed to wriggle and slide under the thorn bushes without doing too much harm to his skin or clothing. And finally, keeping a careful lookout for the five men or any other threats, he and Smudge set off again on their southward journey.

From then on, Malcolm stayed off the main highway. Instead he moved through the countryside well away from the road, with Smudge often circling overhead to make sure he didn't go astray. Only if his way was blocked, by a wall or hedgerow or some other barrier, did he go back on to the road. But he never stayed on it, and was always glad to leave it again.

Yet he was staying off the highway not only to avoid other robbers, but also because he was feeling more and more sad about the wretchedness of the homeless people trudging northward. And his sadness increased with the knowledge that the people wouldn't find things much better in the north, especially if the deadly desert from the Hidden Valley went on spreading and finally caught up with them.

And the land around him was continuing

to show how much worse the drought had become. Day after day the land had kept changing, and it changed even more rapidly over the next few days' travel. In that time Malcolm saw hardly any more stands of woods and not even many lone trees. There were fewer patches of brush, too, except for scatterings of unfriendly briars. The land had opened out into broad, flat grasslands – or what had been grasslands before the drought.

By then, of course, it was a dustbowl, with only rare scattered clumps of brown dry grass to show what it had been. The very soil of the plain, once rich and life-giving, seemed as dead as its grass.

Now and then Malcolm came to a shallow gully or ravine that had once held a small river or a brook, but now held only the dried bodies of small fish, and sun-bleached stones. Or he found a dip or a hollow that had been a pond, now containing only the thin papery remains of frogs. Not even the memory of water remained in those places, not even the ghosts of frogs or fish.

And always, endlessly, a small wind drifted over that plain, stirring the powdery dust into clouds that rose and settled and rose again in a weird lifeless dance. But sometimes the breath of a different wind would gust across the land – a wind from the south, stronger and hotter, as if someone had opened a vast invisible oven. This wind didn't just stir up more of the thin grey dust of the plain. It carried with it a different dust, heavy and gritty, which stung Malcolm's face like grains of harsh dry sand from a desert.

So Malcolm knew, as he walked on and on across the plain, how close he was to the end of his journey – to the spreading desert and the being who had caused it, lurking in the Hidden Valley. But at the same time he wasn't sure exactly *how* near he was, because he didn't know exactly where the Valley lay. And if it really was hidden, he thought, he might walk right past it without knowing, and never find it.

He had thought, earlier, that he would be able to ask the way from people or animals, but there were no other people walking across that dead plain, away from the road, and not many creatures living there. For a while he had seen only insects, and they either didn't understand his question or had never heard of the Valley.

Then, at last, when he was starting to get more anxious, he met a tough, wary crow who did know where the Valley was. In return for some berries, the crow offered to fly up into the air with Smudge and show him the way.

Smudge was far from keen on the idea, but finally agreed. Grumbling, and keeping a safe distance from the crow, he flew high over the plain and looked in the direction the crow pointed. Then he fluttered back down to Malcolm's shoulder, while the crow cawed goodbye and flapped away.

Malcolm waved and turned to Smudge. "So he showed you the way, then?"

" 'E just about showed me the bloomin' *Valley*," Smudge said. "There's a bit of a ridge, sort of low 'ills, like, off that way." He pointed with a wing. "An' beyond the 'ills is the Valley."

Malcolm felt a tightening in his stomach. "We're that near to it, are we?"

"Near ain't the word, Malc," Smudge said gloomily. "By tomorrow mornin', we'll be *there*!"

Chapter 7

Giant Shadow

In fact they nearly got there even sooner. Though Malcolm was feeling tense and nervous, those feelings made him move faster, not slower. It was as if he wanted to get it all over with, to put an end to the time of fretful and fearful travelling. So for the rest of that day, and well past sunset, he kept up a swift and steady pace across the plain, towards the ridge of low hills that Smudge had seen.

Before long he was close enough to see the ridge for himself, through the drifting dust-clouds and the shimmering heat-waves rising from the land. But even before he saw it he knew that he was very close, because the dust around him was no longer fine and powdery and grey. Now its grains were heavy and gritty and brown, not like dry soil but like desert sand.

As twilight began to settle on the bleak landscape, Malcolm could no longer clearly see the change from soil to desert, but he could feel it underfoot as the puffs of soft dust gave way to the grinding slide of sand. And walking on sand is always tiring, so that at last he was forced to stop.

With darkness, the moon rose to show the black mounded shape of the ridge of hills just ahead, with the Hidden Valley waiting beyond them.

"Coo!" Smudge said. He had been dozing on Malcolm's shoulder, but woke as he stopped walking. "We're 'ere. I 'ope you ain't goin' in at *night*, Malc."

"I don't think so," Malcolm said. "The

morning will be soon enough."

He settled down in a little dip in the land, where a deeper drift of sand made a bed. Smudge went back to sleep at once, and despite the nervousness that Malcolm felt, and the hardness of the sandy bed, he was tired enough to fall asleep very quickly as well.

They woke almost at the same time next morning, looking uneasily around. But they could see no danger, no other creatures at all – just the bleak and empty plain, with the ridge of hills jutting up, seeming even closer than they had at night, standing silent as if waiting.

Malcolm grew a bit of fruit for breakfast, and Smudge pecked at the last crumbs from the loaf they had brought, but neither of them was really hungry. Shortly, because there was no point in waiting around, they set off again. And all too soon, feeling a new hollowness in his insides and a shakiness in his knees,

Malcolm climbed a sandy slope to the top of the ridge of hills, then made his way down the other side and into the Hidden Valley.

Some while later, they had moved a fair distance into the Valley and nothing at all had happened. In fact, Malcolm was feeling a bit let down, as if he had been expecting something special to mark their arrival – not just more wind-blown sand, more dry, silent lifelessness.

But at least the Valley was different from the plain they had left behind. It was much more rugged, wrinkled and folded into sloping sandy dunes separated by shallow troughs and gullies. And the land was less bare than the plain had been, with a good many small, twisted trees or low, dark bushes to be seen scattered over the sand. Yet every one of the plants seemed to be utterly dead, the branches reaching out and rattling like the thin dry arms of skeletons.

The problem with the dunes and gullies and brush was that they kept Malcolm from seeing very far ahead, so he was always afraid that he might come face to face with the giant at the top of any slope or behind any bush. Smudge offered to fly above him, to look ahead from the air, but Malcolm didn't think that was a good idea.

"We haven't seen any other birds here at all," he told Smudge. "Maybe they've all left by now. So what if the giant saw you?"

"'E'd never catch me," Smudge said. "'E can't fly, can 'e?"

"Neither can I," Malcolm said. "And if the giant sees you, he might come this way and find me."

"'E might anyway," Smudge muttered. But all the same, he stayed on Malcolm's shoulder and did no flying that morning.

On they went, deeper into the grim depths of the Valley's desert. By then Malcolm was moving more and more slowly, watching all around, peering from the top of every dune, jumping at every wind-swirl of sand – and being startled also by a few creatures that *were* still living in the desert, even though the birds had left.

The creatures that had stayed were those best suited to the dry, harsh and unfriendly surroundings. Malcolm saw lots of flies and other insects, and a good many reptiles. An occasional small lizard would be basking on a flat rock, an occasional small snake would leave its wriggling trail in the sand. Out of curiosity, Malcolm asked one of the lizards how it and its kind managed to survive in such a place.

The lizard regarded him with a cold, unblinking gaze. "We eat insects and small snakes," it said.

"What do the snakes eat?" Malcolm asked.

"Insects and small lizards," said the lizard flatly.

Malcolm nodded and moved on. He had

never much liked talking to reptiles, and the grim savagery of that eat-and-be-eaten desert life made him shudder.

By midday he was feeling tired again, as well as hungry and thirsty, so he found a place to stop, in the shade of a high, oddly-shaped hummock of sand, and grew some oranges and berries for Smudge and himself. Although he enjoyed the rest in the shade, and the welcome juice of the orange, he was also wishing – not for the first time – that he was back home in his cottage, perhaps having a nice egg or two for his lunch.

And Smudge seemed to be feeling the same way, especially since there was not even a crumb left from their loaf. "Wish we'd brought more bread," he grumbled. "Or some bird-seed. I don't much fancy all this *fruit*."

"I could do you a vegetable," Malcolm offered. "Some peas, maybe?"

"Leave it out," Smudge said. "That's no better..." He paused, gazing with interest at the ground. "'Ere, look. We got company."

Malcolm had put his orange peel on the sand while he ate, and it had attracted a number of large, dark ants, streaming out from the hummock of sand, which turned out to be an enormous ant-hill. They were swarming over the peel, apparently paying no attention to anything else, but when Malcolm leaned over and spoke to them in a friendly way, they all went perfectly still for a moment. Then, hurrying away from the peel, they lined up in a neat military row in front of Malcolm.

"We are sorry." As usual with ants, they all spoke together, in one voice, as if they were really just one creature. "We did not know that the fruit-skin belonged to an ant-speaker. Please do not harm us or set your bird on us."

"I wouldn't hurt you," Malcolm assured them. "You're welcome to the peel."

"Wot's that all about?" Smudge wanted to know.

"They're afraid you'll eat them," Malcolm

said with a smile.

"Not me," Smudge said. "Ants taste all 'ot an' sour an' 'orrible." He paused thoughtfully. "Why not ask 'em to 'elp? Maybe they know where the giant is."

"Good idea," Malcolm said, turning back to the ants with the question.

The tidy formation of ants shifted, as if nervous. "The giant's home is very near," they said – which made Malcolm also shift nervously. "But you should stay away from him, ant-speaker. He hunts in the desert every day, and he eats everything he catches. We think he has already eaten another two-legs like you."

"Another—?" Malcolm gasped, horrified. "A *human*?"

"So we believe," the ants said. "One who passed this way a short time ago, who was not an ant-speaker. He had grey fur on his head and face, a long covering on his body, and he held a thin, bright stick."

"The High Wizard!" Malcolm said, feeling sick. "So he *did* get to the Valley! And he's been *eaten*?"

"It must be so," the ants said. "He went towards the giant's home, and he has not been seen again. And the giant eats what he catches."

"But maybe not *people*," Malcolm muttered. And when he told Smudge what had been said, Smudge agreed.

"Ol' wossname, Colcozzen, prob'ly went out of the Valley some other way," the pigeon suggested, "an' no one saw 'im go. 'Oo'd want to eat a wizard anyway?"

Malcolm smiled and turned back to the ants. "Could you tell me where the giant's home is, please?"

"We will gladly *show* you," the ants said, "in return for this fruit-skin."

They all set off together, the line of ants leading the way. By then an enormous stream of other ants was pouring out of the huge ant-hill to gather up the orange peel and any leftover berries. Malcolm took a moment to grow them a few more bushes heavy with berries, smiling again when every one of the hundreds and hundreds of ants said "Thank you very much" at exactly the same time.

But his smile vanished when he followed the ants towards the giant's home. And it was almost chilling, despite the desert heat, to discover just how close he and Smudge had been when they had stopped to eat.

It was just beyond the very next sand dune. There, crouching on the top of that dune, Malcolm found himself staring down into a wide, flat basin of land, with lumps and heaps of bare rock scattered across it, and more dunes and hills rising beyond it.

But the sandy expanse of the basin was not lit up by the glaring sun. Most of it lay in shadow – the shadow cast by the enormous building that was the giant's home.

Chapter 8

Watching and Waiting

It was a huge tower, just as the hawk had said at the start. It reached up and up above the basin of land, its walls looking exactly the same colour as the sand – as if they were actually *made* of sand that had been magically hardened. There were a few narrow shiny windows, but only one door, giant-sized, made from the same strange stone. And from where Malcolm was crouching, it looked as if the door stood slightly open.

They all stared for several moments, but they saw no sign of life anywhere in or around the tower. The building remained as silent as the stony land around it.

"Do you think he's inside?" Malcolm asked the ants.

"We do not know," the ants said. "He often roams the desert by day."

Malcolm watched the tower for another moment, while a cold trickle of sweat ran down his back despite the broiling sun. "We'd better wait around," he said at last, "to see if anything happens."

"Not up on top 'ere," Smudge said. " 'E'd see us right away if 'e came along."

Malcolm swallowed nervously. "Let's go down there, then," he said, pointing to a heap of boulders at one side of the basin, near the tower. "We'd be hidden by those rocks, in the shadow. We might even get a look through the tower's windows."

He began to creep forward, but the ants stopped him. "Wait, ant-speaker!" they cried. "Stay back! The giant has placed magical traps all around his home! They are like huge spider-webs, but they cannot be seen – and they warn him of anyone approaching!"

Malcolm drew back quickly, shaken, wondering whether the High Wizard had run into those invisible traps. "So there's no way to get closer?" he asked the ants.

"Yes, there is," said the ants calmly. "We can sense the webs though we cannot see them. We can show you where you can lie flat and crawl under them, while your bird flies over."

So, with more cold sweat, Malcolm followed the ants, flattening himself where they said, wriggling and creeping his way down from the dune to the cluster of rocks. There he tucked himself into a narrow space between two bulky slabs, where he would be hidden by deeper shadow, even though he was fairly close to the tower's door – which was indeed standing slightly open.

Smudge darted down to join him, feathers

quivering with nervousness, and they both huddled as low as they could in the dark little space. "Thanks for your help," Malcolm whispered to the ants. "We'll probably just wait here now."

"Then we will return home," the ants replied. "Thank you again for the food, ant-speaker. We will gladly help you another time if you need us."

And they marched away in their tidy single file, leaving Malcolm and Smudge alone by the giant's tower.

Time passed. The basin among the dunes baked even dryer in the endless heat, and the sun's fury seemed to smother all sound as well. Now and then Malcolm shifted position or Smudge stretched his wings, to fight stiffness, and the sounds of those small movements seemed terrifyingly loud. Yet nothing happened. The tower's windows remained glassily blank, the door did not move.

More time passed. They grew desperately

thirsty and even felt hungry despite their nervousness. Yet Malcolm did not dare to grow anything with his magic, in case the green of a new plant would be too visible on that dead sand. So they simply stayed still, trying to ignore thirst, hunger, stiffness, the grit in their eyes and the endless fearful anxiety that seemed to be squeezing their insides like icy unseen hands.

And when, after a great deal more time, something finally *did* happen, it came with such unexpected, terrifying suddenness that Malcolm almost yelled aloud with shock, and Smudge might have flown away in panic if he hadn't been too frightened to move.

Without warning, a looming, monstrous figure appeared on top of the ridge on the farther side of the basin.

The giant had returned home.

The soft sand had kept his approach silent, but as he stood on the ridge, the silence ended. He began to bellow in a terrible deep roaring voice. Malcolm and Smudge cowered in their hiding-place, wishing they could turn into grains of sand, certain that the monster was bellowing because he had seen them.

But instead the giant simply strode down the slope towards the door of the tower, still bellowing. And through his fear Malcolm slowly got the idea that the giant might be *singing* – though his voice was so loud and rough and frightening that he couldn't make out the words.

Then the giant stopped singing and stood still, a few paces from the door, and Malcolm's curiosity got the better of his fear. Lifting his head slightly, he took a good look at the enemy.

The giant was at least three times bigger than any man, and at least three times uglier. He wore a long ragged tunic and patched leggings and heavy boots, a huge beard covered most of his lumpy face and his hands were huge and powerful with long dirty nails.

Every bit of him – clothes, skin, hair, everything – seemed to be covered in sand, which never fell off or blew away whatever he did.

Then Malcolm saw, with another icy chill along his spine, that the giant did have one thing that was not sand-covered. Thrust into the wide belt around his tunic was a slender staff, decorated with bright jewels – the magical staff of Colcozzen, the High Wizard.

Even as Malcolm recognized it, wondering sickly if the ants had been right and the wizard had been eaten, he saw the giant take something out of his tunic pocket. It was a glittering jewel, perhaps a diamond, and as big as a football, though it looked small in the giant's hand.

The giant raised the jewel, as if pointing it at the tower's door. Smoothly, the door began to swing wide open.

"Come out!" the giant roared, grinning a huge, ugly grin. "Come out, wizard, and enjoy the nice hot sun!"

And out through the open doorway, floating in mid-air by the power of the giant's magic jewel, came the High Wizard.

He was lying flat as he floated along, so still that at first Malcolm wondered if he was alive. But then he saw the ropes that were wrapped around and around the wizard, binding him tightly. They were very peculiar ropes, too – not only the colour of sand but also somehow grainy and glittery as if they were actually *made* of sand.

And when the magic lowered the wizard to the ground in front of the giant, it was clear that he was very much alive, because his face turned red with anger and he began to shout.

"What are you doing *now*?" he shouted. "I'll tell you once more – let me go at once or you'll regret it!"

The giant laughed, a deep, rough chortle. "You are a fool, wizard. No doubt people leap to obey you, where you come from. But only

I, Drath, give orders here. I will not let you go. Not until you do as I wish and show me how to wield your magical staff."

"You stupid mindless moron of a monster!" Colcozzen raged, so angry that he seemed to forget he was a prisoner. "How often must I say it? The staff will only work for *me*, because it's *mine*!"

The giant stopped him with a roar. "Be silent, fool! You are in no position to insult me! I am Drath, and you will call me no other names or I will leave you where you are to die of thirst and hunger!"

Colcozzen glared and sneered, but seemed at last to see the need for caution. "Very well – *Drath*. But it's true about the staff. No one but myself can wield it. In any case, isn't the power of your diamond enough for you?"

"I have told you," Drath rumbled, "it is no diamond. It is quartz, which is made from lovely sand." He looked fondly at the huge jewel in his hand. "And, yes, its power is enough. It has allowed me to make many fine things from sand – my grand tower, some ropes to bind a wizard… Best of all, it allowed me to capture the clouds, to create a desert."

"Insanity!" Colcozzen muttered.

The giant seemed not to hear him. "A desert that is spreading," he went on. "I have just been out again to look at the edge of the desert, to see how wonderfully *fast* it is spreading. Soon, wizard, as it spreads wider and wider, my magic stone and I will rule this entire world!" His laughter boomed out in savage triumph. "And yet no one can have too much magic, can they? So I want your staff!"

"It's not possible," Colcozzen snapped.

Drath loomed over him, scowling. "You would be wise to think about that, wizard. I must go now to hunt for my supper – and if, when I return, you still refuse to teach me the staff's magic, I may leave you in the desert, where you will add your bones to all the others decorating my sand!"

Raising the jewel, he sent Colcozzen floating back into the tower. Then he wheeled away, bellowing again as he strode across the basin. This time Malcolm knew for certain that Drath was singing, for he could make out the words of the song.

"Sand, lovely sand, so dry in my hand – soon I will spread it all over the land...!"

The terrible noise faded as the giant disappeared over the dunes, striding off into the desert. As silence fell again in the basin, Malcolm could hear angry snarls from Colcozzen, within the tower, as if the wizard was struggling against his magical ropes.

And he could hear those sounds because, with the carelessness of one who fears nothing at all, the giant had again left the tower's door open.

For several moments, crouching in the shadowed hiding-place, Malcolm stared at the open door with a strange light in his eyes. And Smudge, who knew him very well, fluttered his wings uneasily.

"'Ere, Malc," he said at last, "yer not thinkin' wot I think yer thinkin', are you?"

Malcolm didn't take his gaze from the doorway. "I can't just walk away, Smudge," he said.

"Why not?" Smudge demanded. "You came 'ere to see wot's 'appenin', an' now you've seen. Let's go 'ome while we can!"

"When the wizard might be put out on the desert to die?" Malcolm shook his head. "We could never reach any other wizards in time, even if any of them could help..."

"Wot d'you care, after wot 'e did to us before?" Smudge asked angrily. "I bet 'e'd walk away if it was *you* in there!"

"That doesn't make it right for me to go," Malcolm said stubbornly. "I have to try to help him – now, while the giant's not here. I *have* to, Smudge!"

"Yer mad, you are," Smudge said. "The giant could come back any time. An' then what? You couldn't *fight* 'im, Malc. It'd take a whole bloomin' *army* to fight 'im!"

"I wouldn't try," Malcolm said. "I just want to try to help Colcozzen, before Drath gets back. And all this talk is wasting time."

Smudge's wings drooped as he saw Malcolm's determination. "Oh, well, if yer so keen – come on, then. Just try to be quick, awright? An' *careful*, an' all."

Then he hopped up on to Malcolm's shoulder as Malcolm moved slowly and warily forward towards the dark opening of the tower's door.

Chapter 9

Tower of Terror

They paused for another long, shaky moment in the doorway, when Malcolm's legs seemed unwilling to obey his mind. But finally he stumbled through the huge opening into a broad chamber, the whole of the tower's ground floor, which seemed almost empty.

The chamber had only one tall narrow window, which made it dimmer than outside and slightly cooler. Opposite the door a sweeping staircase rose to the upper floors – a staircase made of the same strange sandy stone as the rest of the tower.

The one other thing to be seen in the chamber was quite different. It was a huge square container, like an open box without a lid, which seemed to be made of glass. The glass was thick and heavy and not very smooth, but it was clear enough to see through. And inside the glass box lay the High Wizard.

He was still tightly wrapped in the sandy ropes, lying flat, with plenty of room in the huge box. And he was staring through the glass at Malcolm with a look of total astonishment.

"*You!*" Colcozzen gasped. "How on earth did *you* get here?"

"Walked," Malcolm said briefly, studying the box. The sides weren't very high, he saw, so he thought that if he stretched up as far as he could he might reach quite far down inside.

"Can you sit up a bit?" he said, stretching up over the side. "If I can reach the ropes I might get you loose…"

"Don't be a fool!" Colcozzen snapped. "You couldn't possibly untie these ropes or break them!" He thrashed around, his face red with anger again. "Why did it have to be *you,* with your puny, useless powers? Why couldn't someone come with *real* magic?"

"No one else knows," Malcolm said. "Because you locked me in and I had to escape, and I couldn't tell anyone..."

"Never mind all that!" Colcozzen shouted. "You must *go,* at once – back to the city, to the Wizard School! Bring all the wizards you can find – real wizards with powerful magic! They will be able to free me and deal with the monster!"

"But there's no time!" Malcolm said, startled. "The giant is going to put you out on the desert if you don't tell him about your staff!"

"Nonsense!" Colcozzen spat. "He's always making threats, but he's far too keen on having my staff's magic to harm me. And he won't believe that he can't use it." He glared at Malcolm. "Go on, then! Fetch the wizards!"

"What if they won't come?" Malcolm said doubtfully. "Remember, *you* didn't believe me at first..."

"*Convince* them!" Colcozzen shouted. "Tell them that the giant has a magic stone of great power, and I am in grave danger!" His face was nearly purple with his anger and desperation. "Remember, boy, if anything *does* happen to me, it will be your fault, for not telling the other wizards sooner!"

"That's not fair!" Malcolm said, shocked. "You can't blame me! You should be glad that I'm here at all!"

He turned away angrily towards the door and told Smudge what had been said. The little pigeon flared his wings sharply.

"It'd serve that geezer right," Smudge said hotly, "if we just left 'im an' didn't tell anyone. Come on, let's get out of 'ere. Right, Malc?"

But Malcolm had stopped, and was looking across at the staircase with the strange light in his eyes again.

"It seems a shame," he murmured, "not to have a bit of a look around, while we're here..."

"Malc!" Smudge said pleadingly. "Do us a favour!"

"Just a quick look," Malcolm said, moving towards the stairs. "After all, the *clouds* are supposed to be in here somewhere, Smudge. What if we could find a way to set them free, and end the drought?"

"You! Boy!" It was Colcozzen, shouting furiously again as he saw Malcolm moving away from the door. "What are you doing? I told you to leave at once!"

"So," Malcolm went on, ignoring the wizard's shouts, "I just want to look upstairs for a minute. Then we'll go, Smudge. I promise."

"Awright," Smudge said unhappily. "A *real* quick look..."

They started up the stairs, ignoring Colcozzen's furious ranting. The floor above also held only one broad chamber, which seemed to be a kitchen – messy and filthy and nasty enough to keep Malcolm from inspecting it too closely. The next floor, also one chamber, held nothing except an enormous bed, also made of the same sandy stone as the tower, with a wrinkled blanket and a thick pillow that had the glittery grittiness of the ropes binding Colcozzen, as if even they were magically made of sand.

Finally, carefully, Malcolm and Smudge went up to the next floor, the top floor of the tower. There they saw a short, wide corridor leading to what looked like a blank wall. But when Malcolm went closer, he saw that there was a door set into the wall – a tall, wide door made of the same sandy stone.

No handle or keyhole or hinges or anything could be seen on the door. It fitted so tightly into its frame that only the thinnest of lines showed all the way around it. But even so, it was not quite tight enough to stifle the strange sounds that were coming faintly through from the chamber beyond the door.

At first Malcolm couldn't believe he was hearing them. They would have been unlikely sounds anywhere in all the drought-stricken land, but they were especially unlikely in a stony tower in the middle of a desert. For they were *wet* sounds – a mingling harmony of moist sighings, bubbly rumblings, soft drippings, small splashings...

"The *clouds*," Malcolm whispered, wide-eyed.

He pressed his ear to the door, listening hard, licking his dry lips as the watery sounds reminded him of how thirsty he was. Then he reached out, trying to jam his fingernails into the thin crack around the door's edge, as if he had the wild notion that he could pull the door open by force.

But the door was so tight that he couldn't even begin to get a grip. All that happened was that a tiny fleck of the stone, no more than one grain of the sand it was made from, came away under one of his fingernails.

"You 'opin' to break it down bare-'anded?" Smudge asked, as Malcolm peered glumly at the speck of sand. "You don't even know 'ow thick it is. It'd prob'ly take you for ever to get through even if you 'ad 'ammers an' chisels an' that."

"I suppose," Malcolm said thoughtfully. "But if I had help…"

"Wot 'elp?" Smudge scoffed. "Like I said before about fightin' the giant – you'd need a bloomin' *army*."

Malcolm nodded. And then another strange light appeared in his eyes, and he began to smile. But before he could tell Smudge about the brilliant idea that had come to him, he was silenced.

A huge bellowing voice rose up the stairway

from below. A voice that seemed to be trying to sing.

"Sand, lovely sand, isn't it grand..."

The giant was home again.

Smudge gave a bubbling cry and leaped from Malcolm's shoulder, flying up to the ceiling in sudden panic. Malcolm pressed himself back against the wall in a panic of his own, his legs feeling like ice-cold jelly. But Smudge's terrified flapping somehow shook his mind back into action again.

"Sssh!" he hissed desperately. "Come on – we have to *hide*!"

Smudge came back to his shoulder, every feather quivering with fear. "'Ide? Where?"

Malcolm thought frantically. "One floor down – under the bed!"

And he dashed to the stairs – while, below, the giant's voice boomed as he spoke to Colcozzen.

"See how lucky I was, wizard!" Drath was

saying. "Five fat lizards and as many snakes, only a short way from my door! They will make a fine dinner!" His laughter rose. "I may even give you some, if you agree to teach me the use of your staff!"

He had clearly forgotten about his threat to leave the wizard in the desert. And Colcozzen, in turn, had clearly forgotten how unwise it was to be rude to a giant, while tied up.

"Keep your dinner!" he snarled. "I'm sick of your filthy food, and I'm sick of your ignorant blather about the staff!"

The giant growled angrily. "Ignorant, am I? Very well, you will do without dinner. We will see what you say when you have starved a little." His grin was ugly and cruel. "Remember, wizard, I am in no hurry. When my desert has spread over everything, everywhere, I will have all the time in the *world!*"

Meanwhile Malcolm had sped silently down into the giant's bedroom. Holding

Smudge comfortingly against his chest, he slid under the massive stony bed. And then he froze as if he too had turned to stone, when he heard Drath's next words.

"No need to hurry with dinner either," he said with a loud, grunting yawn. "I will leave you to think about what is in store for you, wizard, while I have a nice little nap."

And Malcolm heard the clumping of his giant boots as he started up the stairs towards his bedroom.

Chapter 10

Captives

"Quick!" Malcolm gasped, scrambling out from under the bed and leaping for the door, still holding Smudge. His idea was to go down one floor again, before the giant came up to it, and find a hiding-place in the messy kitchen. Then the giant would go on past, he hoped, up to the bedroom, and Malcolm and Smudge could sneak out later.

It almost worked. He fled down the stairs, with Smudge fluttering against his chest, and made it into the kitchen before the giant had come up that far. But as he rushed across the room, looking for a place to hide behind one of the smelly counters, his foot landed on something nasty and greasy – and skidded out from under him.

He fell with a thumping crash against a cabinet, rattling several huge stained pans.

Winded and bruised, he tried to leap up quickly, still clinging to Smudge. But before he found his feet, the room was filled with a mighty roar that nearly knocked him over again.

Drath loomed in the doorway, astounded and furious, pulling his magic jewel from his tunic pocket.

"What is this?" he bellowed. "A *thief* sneaking around my kitchen? No more sneaking for you, thief!"

He held up the jewel. At once Malcolm felt something thin and strong, like rope, wrapping itself around him. It was the same sort of sandy rope that held Colcozzen, and Malcolm barely had time to let Smudge go before he was completely wrapped up, like a cocoon, unable to move.

He toppled to the floor with a gasp as Smudge flew into the air. Then, astonishingly, the little pigeon wheeled and flew back down, like a small grey missile, at the giant's face. Drath growled and slapped at him as a man might swipe at a fly, but Smudge dodged the huge hand and swung around to launch another attack.

"*No*, Smudge!" Malcolm yelled, finally finding his voice. "Get *away*! Fly back to the desert, to our friends! Bring *help!*"

At once Smudge swooped away, flashing out through the door. Malcolm held his breath, wondering if Drath would use the jewel to capture the pigeon too, but the giant merely turned to him with a brutal grin.

"Stop your blubbering," he growled. "You seem more frightened than your little pet."

Malcolm took a deep breath and lay still. Of course, pigeon language just sounded like wordless tearful cries to Drath. Smudge was safely away and perhaps the idea really would work…

He jerked with shock as he felt his bound body rise from the floor and float out of the kitchen, lifted by the jewel's power.

"Come, little thief," Drath rumbled, setting off downstairs again with Malcolm floating beside him. "Come and meet a wizard. Then you can tell us both where you found the courage to sneak into *my* home."

On the ground floor, Malcolm saw that Colcozzen was glaring furiously from the glass box where he was held. "You brainless fool!" Colcozzen shouted. "If you had left when I told you to, you would be safely away now, able to go for help! Now look what you have done!"

Drath chortled, using the jewel to lower Malcolm into the glass box, beside the wizard. "So the plan was for the thief to go for help, was it? What sort of help did you hope for?"

Once again, Colcozzen's anger got in the way of thought. "If the idiot had done as he was told, he would have brought *wizards* to deal with you, rather than his own pathetic magic..."

Then he saw Drath begin to smile and realized too late that he had said too much. And the giant roared with laughter.

"So he is magical as well!" Drath laughed. "And now I have *two* of you to learn more magic from!"

As his laughter rolled out again, Malcolm glared at Colcozzen, feeling too angry to be afraid any more. "You know, High Wizard," he said through clenched teeth, "you talk too much. Why don't you just keep quiet?"

Colcozzen twitched furiously within his bonds, but before he could begin an outraged reply, the giant stopped him.

"A good idea, young one," he chortled. "I too am tired of his self-important voice."

He raised the jewel, and a band of the

magical sandy rope appeared from nowhere to wrap itself around the shocked wizard's mouth.

"He may remain like that," Drath went on, "until he is ready to tell me the secrets of his staff." His chortling gave way to a huge yawn. "Now I will have my nap, at last, and then my dinner, and later we will talk some more. Till then, you may enjoy the peace and quiet."

Chortling and yawning, he clumped away towards the stairs.

Malcolm looked at Colcozzen. The wizard's face was purplish-red once again as he strained helplessly against the sandy ropes that held him, glaring at Malcolm in a towering fury.

"I'm sorry," Malcolm said. "I didn't know he'd do that."

The gagged wizard went on glaring, but Malcolm turned away, forcing himself to be calm, gazing longingly at the half-open door. He knew that it would take Smudge some time to get where he was going – and it would probably take even longer for the pigeon to gather the help that he had gone to find. As he had nothing else to do, Malcolm went on watching the door, hoping for his friend's return.

Time crept slowly by through the afternoon. The giant awoke from his nap and clumped down from his bedroom to the kitchen, where pans clattered and nasty, greasy cooking smells began to float down the stairway. Shortly afterwards, Drath lumbered down to the ground floor, holding out a large blackened pan that was sizzling slightly.

"Some food for you, young one," Drath boomed. "The wizard may stay hungry, so that his mouth can stay shut." He chortled, holding out the pan towards Malcolm. "You will find the broiled lizard quite tender."

Malcolm drew back, trying not to look as sick as he felt. "Um … I'm not all that hungry," he said. "I'd really just like a drink."

"Of course." The giant reached into his tunic, bringing out a flask made of a brownish glass, and leaned down to offer it to Malcolm. "Do you not like the lovely glass that I make from my sand?"

Malcolm jerked his head back from the horrible stink rising out of the flask. "What's *in* there?" he gasped.

"Lizard blood, of course," Drath said with a frown. "With some snake venom, to add flavour. Though the wizard has never liked it much..."

"Really," Malcolm said weakly, "I ... I'd just as soon have a drink of water."

The giant stiffened, drawing himself up to his full height, his face becoming an enormous mask of outrage. "You *dare*?" he bellowed. "You will speak that word to me in my own home? Foul-mouthed vermin! I will not stand here and be insulted by such vileness!"

Malcolm shrank back, afraid that he would

be attacked. But instead, to his great surprise, Drath merely wheeled and marched away in a temper, stamping heavily up the stairs.

Huddling down on the floor of the cage, Malcolm didn't even look at Colcozzen, who was sure to be glaring. I should have known, he thought unhappily. Of course *water* would be disgusting to a giant who is so keen on desert sand and dryness.

He went on huddling there, wrapped in the ropes, so miserable that he hardly noticed how hungry and thirsty he was. And he stayed like that as time passed, and night came down on to the desert to darken the tower windows and the open door. That made him even more miserable, since of course Smudge couldn't fly after dark, and wouldn't be able to get back to the tower before daylight. If he comes at all, Malcolm thought unhappily. He might have had an accident, or anything.

With such thoughts filling his mind, he was

certain that he would never be able to sleep in the glass box. But as the night wore on he did begin to doze, and then to sleep more deeply. And he was in the middle of the same nightmare about being buried by a sand dune – feeling the grains of sand trickling over his face – when the sound of a familiar voice awoke him with a jolt.

"Wakey, wakey, Malc," said Smudge's voice. "Let's be 'avin' you."

Malcolm opened his eyes, delighted to see Smudge perched on the side of the glass box in the early morning light. Then he saw Colcozzen staring at him with distaste, and he realized why.

There were about a dozen large ants crawling over him, and one of them was walking across his cheek, its delicate feet feeling like the grains of sand in his dream.

It came to a stop, gazing intently into his right eye. "Good morning, ant-speaker," it said, with the other eleven ants speaking at the same time, as usual. "Your bird seemed to want us to come to you."

"Yes, thank you," Malcolm said warmly. "I'm glad you're here." He glanced at Smudge. "I'm glad you made it too, Smudge. Was it all right?"

Smudge flicked his tail. "Nothin' to it. I thought I'd 'ave trouble makin' 'em understand, but they're sort of bright, for bugs."

And when Malcolm explained his problem, and his idea, the ants again seemed to understand very quickly. The one on his cheek scurried down to join the others, inspecting the magical ropes.

"It should not be difficult," they said at last. "It is just *sand*, though it has been greatly hardened. And ants know how to dig in sand."

"The trouble is," Malcolm told them, "I don't know how much time you'd have. And then there's the door on the top floor, which is probably a lot thicker than the ropes..."

"Perhaps we should go for reinforcements," the ants said. "With more workers, the work would go swiftly."

"I'd be very grateful," Malcolm said. "And I'd grow food for you all, in return – as much as you could eat."

The twelve ants twitched their antennae. "If you are willing to do that, ant-speaker, we will gather all the ants of the desert to help you!"

"That's it!" Malcolm said eagerly. "That's what we need, just like Smudge said before. Bring an *army*!"

Chapter 11

The Army Marches

"'Ang on!" Smudge said, when Malcolm told him the plan. "You 'aven't got all day! Wot's the giant gonna be doin' while yer waitin' for this lot to crawl all the way back to their ant-'eap an' then bring their mates crawlin' all the way back 'ere again?"

"I know," Malcolm said, "but we need all the ants..." He paused as a new idea came to him. "What if only one or two went back, while the others stayed and got started? And what if those two *flew* back?"

"They ain't flyin' ants," Smudge objected.

Then he drew back warily. "'Ere! D'you mean wot I think you mean?"

"You could carry two ants," Malcolm said pleadingly. "And I'm sure they'd be willing..."

"I ain't a passenger pigeon, am I?" Smudge grumbled. "But ... awright, I'll try it. As long as they 'old tight an' keep *still*. I don't want 'em skitterin' around in my feathers like oversize bloomin' fleas."

The ants were a bit startled when Malcolm put the idea to them, but they saw how much time would be gained, and agreed. Two of them climbed on to Smudge's back, making him twitch a little, then took a firm grip on his feathers with their jaws. And Smudge whisked away, through the door.

Meanwhile, the ten remaining ants set to work, using their jaws in a quite different way. They began biting at one particular spot on one rope, where it crossed Malcolm's left arm. They bit at it one after another, in turn, each bite taking one small fleck of sand away from the rough surface of the rope.

At first Malcolm watched with eager hope. But he soon began to feel anxious, for though the ants bit and bit at the rope for quite some while, they seemed to be having no effect on it at all.

Still, ants are tireless workers, and are incredibly strong for their size, with particularly powerful jaws. Before much more time had passed, as they gnawed away at the rope without slowing or faltering, Malcolm found that he could see a definite mark on that one spot on the rope – a shallow scratch, the beginnings of a gouge.

Time went on, the sun shone more brightly through the narrow window, and the ants worked on with no signs of weariness or boredom. At one point the monotony was broken by a moment of terror, when Malcolm heard a rumbling sound from the giant's bedroom. But then he relaxed, realizing that

Drath was only snoring. He was clearly not an early riser, and Malcolm nervously hoped he would have a nice long lie-in.

Some while after that, when Malcolm was again gazing longingly at the open doorway, the waiting came to an end, and tedium turned into tension once again.

"There, ant-speaker," said the ants. "What shall we do now?"

Malcolm looked down. At that one spot over his left arm, the hard magical rope had been completely chewed through, leaving two ragged ends.

"That's terrific!" he said to the ants. And he began to try to move that arm, straining against the other ropes that still encircled him.

But then he halted in sudden fright. From above, he heard a heavy rustling and thumping, a huge gusty yawn, and then the sounds of great boots thudding on the stairs. The giant was on his way down.

"Good morning!" Drath boomed as he

reached the ground floor, smiling cheerfully, as if he had forgotten his anger of the night before. "Is it not a lovely, hot, dry day?"

Malcolm shrank back, terrified that Drath would come closer and see the damaged rope. And in his near-panic he hit upon a highly risky way to keep the giant at a distance.

"It's *too* dry!" he said loudly. "I want a drink of *water*!"

As before, Drath stopped and seemed to swell with rage. "You speak that foul word to me again?" he roared. "I warn you, if I hear it once more I will bind your mouth as I have the wizard's!"

In his fury he wheeled and stamped away, just as Malcolm had hoped. In fact he stamped out of the tower, leaving the door carelessly open as usual, and Malcolm listened gleefully to the sound of his footsteps fading away outside.

"He's probably gone hunting," he told the ants. "That gives us some time..."

As he spoke, he was trying again to move his left arm, straining against the broken rope. At first nothing happened, but then with a startling suddenness the broken ends of the rope pulled farther apart. With that, every one of the other ropes began to unwind and untangle, slipping loose, falling away. And Malcolm got to his feet in the glass box, delightedly free.

Quickly he climbed over the side of the box, then turned back to look at Colcozzen. The wizard had stopped glaring, and was looking both amazed and hopeful. But Malcolm slowly shook his head.

"Sorry," he said. "There's no time to let you loose now. And I don't much want you around shouting and giving orders and getting in the way."

Colcozzen glared again, thrashing, grunting and gurgling behind his gag, but Malcolm turned away. Taking a deep breath, gathering every scrap of his courage, he set off towards the stairs with the group of ants in line behind him.

He had taken only a step or two when Smudge came hurtling in through the open door, wheeling around the chamber. And Malcolm went rigid with fright, for it seemed that Smudge was being pursued by a gigantic, buzzing, storming cloud of flying insects that filled the room.

The pigeon landed on his shoulder, bubbling with excitement. "The ants are comin'," he announced breathlessly. "An' they've only gone an' rounded up just about every other bug in the desert, an' all. They sent the flyin' ones ahead, with me, to get started. The rest'll be 'ere soon."

"Terrific!" Malcolm cried, staring at the vast, swarming cloud. He saw locusts and winged beetles and a few hornets, but that was about all he could recognize. Still, he knew, they would all be tough and hardy insects, or they wouldn't be able to live in the desert. And that was the kind he needed.

"Come on!" he called, using the locust language and hoping the others would understand. "We have to break through a door!"

He leaped up the stairs, with the flying insects swarming after him and the small troop of ants following more slowly. At the top of the stairs, they all gathered in the corridor by the great door where the clouds were imprisoned. And when Malcolm had carefully explained what had to be done, the insects went to work.

Malcolm had picked a spot at the edge of the door, along the narrow tight seam where the door fitted into its frame. There, without hesitation, the insects began to bite at the stone, just as the troop of ants had gnawed Malcolm's rope. One at a time, steadily, the locusts and beetles and all the others bit tiny grains of sand away from the rough surface of the stone.

"Wot's this?" Smudge asked, watching. "They gonna chew up the door or somethin'?"

"Not the whole door," Malcolm said. "That'd take for ever. They just need to make a *hole*. Clouds are sort of like steam, so it doesn't even need to be a big hole to let them out."

"Just as well," Smudge said. "It might take for ever anyway, the way they're goin'."

That seemed true, Malcolm thought unhappily. The insects were willing enough, and there were thousands of them. But they weren't all natural workers like ants, nor did they all have such strong jaws. By then the small troop of ants had reached the top floor and had set to work gnawing at the opposite edge of the door, and the whole swarm of flying insects didn't seem to be having much more effect than those few ants.

But before Malcolm could grow any more anxious, his spirits were lifted by the arrival of the rest of the ants. They were, as he had hoped, an immense army, marching along in soldierly fashion – with scuttling beetles, hopping sand fleas and crawlers of many other sorts among them. There were so many of them in that mighty army that they looked like an enormous living carpet, pouring up the stairs.

"Infantry's 'ere!" Smudge said merrily.

"Wonderful!" Malcolm breathed.

"We have promised there will be food for all, ant-speaker," said the ants, "if you can manage it. But first, we will work."

And at once the ants and the other newcomers began to attack the door, at the spot where the first group of ten ants had begun, while the flying insects went on working at the door's other edge.

Yet even then Malcolm's worries weren't over. After a time it seemed that neither swarm of insects was making much headway. Perhaps the sandstone of the door was harder than the rope had been, he thought. And the flying insects seemed to be slowing down, as if they were losing interest.

"No," a locust said to Malcolm, when he asked. "We are just getting tired. We are not used to such work, as ants are. We need food, to restore us."

"Is that all?" said Malcolm with a relieved smile. "Then it's time for a dinner break."

And he began, magically, to grow heavily laden berry bushes on the bare stone of the floor.

Some were tall bushes – blackberry or raspberry – for the flying insects, with lower kinds like blueberry and strawberry for the crawling ones. The first lot of bushes was stripped of the ripe fruit almost at once, by the hungry workers, so Malcolm exerted himself and grew more. And when those berries had gone too, the insects all went energetically back to work on the door.

That was when Malcolm noticed an

interesting thing. He knew, of course, that even quite delicate plants are able to damage stone, when their roots and stems grow through it. And that was exactly what had happened. The tough roots of the berry bushes had made small webbed networks of cracks in the stone floor where they had been grown.

"Hang on!" Malcolm called to the insects. "I think I can help make things go faster!"

And though he was tired from growing the bushes, he fixed his gaze on the edges of the door, and worked his magic.

Grass began to sprout where the insects were working – tough, coarse grass, with long, strong, tangled roots.

And as the grass grew, small networks of cracks began to appear at the edges of the door.

At once the insects flung themselves back to work. In no time, as they bit and tore at the tiny cracks in the stone, more and more of the door's edges began to flake away. By then it was clear that the door *was* very thick – but even so, grinning with delight despite his tiredness and anxiety, Malcolm simply went on growing grass, around and under the army of insect workers.

Until they ran out of time.

The mighty bellow from the bottom of the stairs seemed to shake the tower, and almost made Malcolm leap out of his boots with fright.

Drath was back, and berserk with fury.

"*Gone?*" he was bellowing. "*Escaped?* He cannot escape! He will regret this when I find him!"

Malcolm held his breath, shaking with fear. And all the flying insects came away from the door, sensing danger, and buzzed around him in a huge swirling cloud.

There was no chance that the sound would not be heard, even downstairs. And again the tower seemed to tremble, with Drath's raging bellow and the pounding of his giant boots, as he came charging up the stairs.

Chapter 12

The Victory

Malcolm's heart seemed to stop with terror, and his feet were rooted to the floor like the berry bushes. But as the giant came thundering up, the clouds of flying insects stormed down the corridor to meet him, swirling around his head in an angry frenzy.

The giant halted his charge, roaring, swatting at the vast cloud of winged things. And then he swatted again – at Smudge, who had leaped from Malcolm's shoulder with a pigeon battle-cry, darting at Drath's face.

The giant's flailing hand brushed against Smudge as he dived. Though it was only a glancing blow, it slammed the little pigeon against the wall with brutal force. And Malcolm cried out in horror as he saw Smudge drop to the floor, silent and limp.

Then Malcolm yelled again, with a wild anger that swept away all his fear. The giant was still pawing at the cloud of insects, staring with shock at the vast army of ants and other creatures massed on the wall and the door. With another roar, he pulled the magical gemstone from his tunic pocket. But before he could use its power, Malcolm called on every last bit of his own small magic, and attacked.

As Drath leaped towards him along the corridor, holding up the great jewel, Malcolm's magic covered the floor at his feet with a very special plant. It was a thin green lichen, smooth and slightly slimy, which on a flat surface was terribly slippery.

The giant's feet slid out from under him and he fell with an enormous crash. And as he hit the floor, the gemstone slipped from his hand and bounced away.

"*Get him!*" Malcolm shouted in several insect languages. And the army did as he asked.

The huge cloud of flying things zoomed down upon Drath, covering him, buzzing into his eyes and mouth, biting him, stinging him if they had stingers. And as the giant bellowed and flailed, slipping again on the lichen as he tried to get to his feet, Malcolm kicked the big gemstone into the tangle of berry bushes, and began to grow more plants.

A jungle of long thorny vines arose, wrapping around Drath as he struggled, holding him down. Though Drath fought with all his giant strength, tearing and snapping the vines that bound him, Malcolm simply grew more. In among the vines he also grew thick stout bushes with thorns like daggers – he grew a spreading, coiling network of wiry brambles – he grew nettles and thistles, poison ivy and poison oak.

And yet, although Drath was bruised and stung and poisoned and entangled, he fought with enormous, raging power, tearing aside every barrier that Malcolm made. Malcolm could feel himself growing even more tired from working his magic non-stop. And when his strength gave out, he knew, Drath would win.

But he pushed that thought away and fought on, throwing up a new briar patch in front of the raging giant, racking his brains to think of some other way to defeat the monster. Yet Drath was still crashing through the barriers, still forcing his way along the corridor one slow step at a time, seeming tireless and unstoppable, despite everything that Malcolm was doing.

And then, as Malcolm fell back wearily from the giant's advance, two completely astounding things happened at the same time.

He felt the flutter of small wings by his ear, felt small claws grip his shoulder. "Coo!" Smudge said. " 'E knocked me lights right out for a minute, the big 'ooligan!"

And as Malcolm began to turn to his friend with a glad cry, he heard another voice. It was the loud and slightly startled voice of all the ants – who had been going dutifully and tirelessly on with their work on the door, despite the battle raging in the corridor.

"Look, ant-speaker!" cried the ants.

Malcolm looked – and saw, at the spot on the door's edge where the army of ants had been biting, a tiny, drifting wisp of something that looked like smoke.

But it wasn't smoke. And at once it was also no longer tiny. As a force from the other side of the door thrust powerfully against the pin-sized hole that the ants had made, the stone began to crumble more rapidly, and the opening grew larger.

And in a blasting, rushing jet like steam under high pressure, with a mighty hissing sound full of joy and triumph, the clouds escaped.

Drath's raging bellows suddenly turned into terrified howls as the clouds gushed out. But Malcolm could no longer see his giant enemy, for the clouds had filled the corridor like heavy, cool fog. And as more and more clouds escaped, the fogginess was thickened even more by a downpour of misty rain.

The cool wetness was a wonderful feeling on Malcolm's skin, but he had no time to pause and enjoy it. He could see that, as the soft rain began to soak the walls and floors of the corridor, it was having an unexpected and frightening effect.

The magical sandstone was melting.

"*Run!*" he shouted to the insects.

Seeing the danger, all of his small allies rushed for the stairs, with Smudge flapping overhead. There was still no sign of Drath, whose howls had become oddly shrill and had then stopped entirely. But Malcolm had no wish to stay around to find out what had happened. Skidding on the slippery lichen, he hurtled down the stairs.

By then the clouds had also found the way out and were sweeping wetly down the stairs all around him. And when Malcolm reached the ground floor, he saw that the rain had done its work there as well. The glass box and the ropes binding the High Wizard had been melted away, and Colcozzen was standing in a puddle, staring around in shock.

Malcolm grabbed the wizard's arm and dragged him outside to join Smudge and the insect army. And as Smudge and the insects streamed out to join them, they stood watching the tower. Malcolm saw the great main door fall away into a muddy heap, after which the doorway's opening also vanished as the wall above it sagged. All the walls were slumping, losing their form and firmness as the cool rain kept falling. Finally, with a strange, thick, squelchy, sighing sound, the entire remaining mass of the tower fell in upon itself, becoming nothing more than a vast shapeless mound of soggy sand, like an oversized sandcastle drowned by a rising tide.

By then the clouds had spread out over all the Hidden Valley and the land beyond it, veiling the sun's hot glare, pouring their healing rain on to the grateful earth.

"We *did* it, Malc!" Smudge burbled. "The drought's over!"

"I don't understand," Malcolm said dazedly. "Why couldn't the clouds escape *before*, if they could melt the stone?"

Colcozzen tugged at his beard, also looking dazed. "I would think that Drath made an even *harder* stone for the room where he put the clouds. And he may have strengthened it regularly with magic."

"It was hard stone, all right," Malcolm

agreed. "Nearly too hard."

Without replying, Colcozzen suddenly clambered up on top of the sludgy mound of sand that was all that was left of the tower. Malcolm followed, watching curiously as the wizard scrabbled around among the leftover vines and brush. Then he straightened up, holding his jewelled staff that had been tucked into the giant's belt.

In the same moment Smudge flashed away from Malcolm's shoulder, diving down among the clutter of vines and coming up with another prize. In his beak he was gripping a tiny being, no bigger than a locust. As it struggled feebly, shrieking in a thin little voice, Malcolm and Colcozzen stared in new amazement.

The tiny thing was Drath.

"So *that's* why he's magical!" the wizard said with satisfaction. "He's not really a giant at all. He's some kind of *gnome*."

He raised his staff and murmured a strange

word. In his other hand there appeared a delicate, shiny object – a small box made of smooth, clear glass with several air-holes in its lid.

"We'll see how *he* likes it in a glass box," Colcozzen snapped, taking the tiny wriggling Drath from Smudge and dropping him into the box. "Now then, gnome," the wizard went on sternly, "explain yourself."

Shakily, fearfully, in his shrill little voice, Drath explained. He was a *sand-gnome*, who had found the magic gemstone in a cavern below the earth, and had used it to make his own gnomish magic more powerful. With the jewel he had turned himself into a giant, able to make almost anything he wished out of sand.

But he had known that the magic would work only if he, and the jewel, and his magical creations, never came into contact with water. So he had stolen the clouds, to dry up the land and keep it from ever raining again.

"What do we do with him now?" Malcolm asked, peering at the tiny figure cowering in the glass box.

Colcozzen scowled. "His jewel has been melted in the rain, like everything else. But Drath himself must be put somewhere that will keep him out of trouble. I think … yes, a nice watery *swamp* would be an ideal place. There's a nice muddy, rainy, boggy one in the far north…"

He raised his staff and spoke some words, and the tiny figure of Drath the sand-gnome vanished, flung by the wizard's magic into the faraway swamp where he could never get into trouble again.

Malcolm said goodbye, with heartfelt thanks, to the insect army, waving as they set off cheerfully across the rain-cooled desert.

"It's going to take a long time for this valley to come back to life," he said quietly. "And the rest of the land, too."

"We wizards will help," Colcozzen said. "We'll do whatever we can to overcome the effects of the drought." He cleared his throat, looking ill at ease and embarrassed. "And now, ah, Malcolm … I have … I must … I think I owe you … an apology."

"All right," Malcolm said easily.

"No, no," Colcozzen said. "I was wrong to belittle your … unusual magic. You have shown me that smaller powers, and smaller creatures, can do great and heroic things, even where larger powers have failed. I owe you an apology, and the land owes you a great deal more. I shall see to it that your heroism is rewarded."

"All right," Malcolm said again. "But now I'd just like to get home."

"Of course," the wizard said. "I'll take you home by magic, in a twinkling. But later, I hope you will come to the city again. It's clear that we were wrong to keep you out of the Wizard School, and I'd like you to join now.

Not to *study*," he added hastily, as Malcolm frowned, "but to *teach*, so that the trainee wizards may learn the value of your sort of magic."

"I don't know," Malcolm said. "I wouldn't want to do it all the time. I've got my house and garden to look after. And my friends..."

"Whenever you wish," Colcozzen said, beaming.

"Come on, Malc," Smudge interrupted. "We goin' to stay 'ere all day?" He nudged Malcolm with a wing. "Alice might be waitin', y' know."

And so Colcozzen raised his staff, wrapped them in a bright globe of magic, and carried them back towards home through the steady downpour of healing rain.

Goosebumps

by R.L. Stine

Reader beware, you're in for a scare!

These terrifying tales will send shivers up your spine . . .

Available now:

1 **Welcome to Dead House**
2 **Say Cheese and Die!**
3 **Stay out of the Basement**
4 **The Curse of the Mummy's Tomb**
5 **Monster Blood**
6 **Let's Get Invisible**
7 **Night of the Living Dummy**
8 **The Girl Who Cried Monster**
9 **Welcome to Camp Nightmare**
10 **The Ghost Next Door**
11 **The Haunted Mask**
12 **Piano Lessons Can Be Murder**
13 **Be Careful What You Wish For**
14 **The Werewolf of Fever Swamp**
15 **You Can't Scare Me**
16 **One Day at Horrorland**
17 **Why I'm Afraid of Bees**
18 **Monster Blood II**
19 **Deep Trouble**
20 **Go Eat Worms**

Look out for:

21 **Return of the Mummy**
22 **The Scarecrow Walks at Midnight**
23 **Attack of the Mutant**

Our favourite Babysitters are detectives too! Don't miss the new series of Babysitters Club Mysteries:

Available now:

No 1: Stacey and the Missing Ring
When Stacey's accused of stealing a valuable ring from a new family she's been sitting for, she's devastated – Stacey is *not* a thief!

No 2: Beware, Dawn!
Just *who* is the mysterious "Mr X" who's been sending threatening notes to Dawn and phoning her while she's babysitting, *alone*?

No 3: Mallory and the Ghost Cat
Mallory thinks she's solved the mystery of the spooky cat cries coming from the Craine's attic. But Mallory can *still* hear crying. Will Mallory find the *real* ghost of a cat this time?

No 4: Kristy and the Missing Child
When little Jake Kuhn goes missing, Kristy can't stop thinking about it. Kristy makes up her mind. She *must* find Jake Kuhn . . . wherever he is!

No 5: Mary Anne and the Secret in the Attic
Mary Anne is curious about her mother, who died when she was just a baby. Whilst rooting around in her creepy old attic Mary Anne comes across a secret she never knew . . .

No 6: The Mystery at Claudia's House
Just what is going on? Who has been ransacking Claudia's room and borrowing her make-up and clothes? Something strange is happening at Claudia's house and the Babysitters are determined to solve the mystery . . .

No 7: Dawn and the Disappearing Dogs
Dawn decides to try her hand at *pet*sitting for a change, and feels terrible when one of her charges just . . . disappears. But when other dogs in the neighbourhood go missing, the Babysitters know that someone is up to no good . . .

No 8: Jessi and the Jewel Thieves
Jessi is thrilled to be taking a trip to see Quint in New York, and thinks that nothing could be more exciting. But when they overhear a conversation between jewel thieves, she knows that the adventure has only just begun . . .

No 9: Kristy and the Haunted Mansion
Travelling home from a game, Kristy and her all-star baseball team are stranded when a huge storm blows up. The bridges collapse, and the only place they can stay looks – haunted . . .

Look out for:

No 10: Stacey and the Mystery Money
No 11: Claudia and the Mystery at the Museum
No 12: Dawn and the Surfer Ghost

THE UNDERWORLD TRILOGY
Peter Beere

When life became impossible for the homeless of London many left the streets to live beneath the earth. They made their homes in the corridors and caves of the Underground. They gave their home a name. They called it UNDERWORLD.

UNDERWORLD
It was hard for Sarah to remember how long she'd been down there, but it sometimes seemed like forever. It was hard to remember a life on the outside. It was hard to remember the real world. Now it seemed that there was nothing but creeping on through the darkness, there was nothing but whispering and secrecy.

And in the darkness lay a man who was waiting to kill her . . .

UNDERWORLD II
"Tracey," she called quietly. No one answered. There was only the dark threatening void which forms Underworld. It's a place people can get lost in, people can disappear in. It's not a place for young girls whose big sisters have deserted them. Mandy didn't know what to do. She didn't know what had swept her sister and her friends from Underworld. All she knew was that Tracey had gone off and left her on her own.

UNDERWORLD III
Whose idea was it? Emma didn't know and now it didn't matter anyway. It was probably Adam who had said, "Let's go down and look round the Underground." It was something to tell their friends about, something new to try. To boast that they had been inside the secret Underworld, a place no one talked about, but everyone knew was there.

It had all seemed like a great adventure, until they found the gun . . .

Also by Peter Beere

CROSSFIRE
When Maggie runs away from Ireland, she finds herself roaming the streets of London destitute and alone. But Maggie has more to fear then the life of a runaway. Her step-father is an important member of the IRA – and if he doesn't find her before his enemies do, Maggie might just find herself caught up in the crossfire . . .

Encounter worlds where men and women make hazardous voyages through space; where time travel is a reality and the fifth dimension a possibility; where the ultimate horror has already happened and mankind breaks through the barrier of technology . . .

The Obernewtyn Chronicles:
Book 1: Obernewtyn
Book 2: The Farseekers
Isobelle Carmody
A new breed of humans are born into a hostile world struggling back from the brink of apocalypse . . .

Random Factor
Jessica Palmer
Battle rages in space. War has been erased from earth and is now controlled by an all-powerful computer – until a random factor enters the system . . .

First Contact
Nigel Robinson
In 1992 mankind launched the search for extra-terrestial intelligence. Two hundred years later, someone responded . . .

Virus
Molly Brown
A mysterious virus is attacking the staff of an engineering plant . . . Who, or *what* is responsible?

Look out for:

Strange Orbit
Margaret Simpson

Scatterlings
Isobelle Carmody

Body Snatchers
Stan Nicholls

Read Point SF and enter a new dimension . . .

Point Romance

Caroline B. Cooney

The lives, loves and hopes of five young girls appear in this dazzling mini series:

Anne – coming to terms with a terrible secret that has changed her whole life.

Kip – everyone's best friend, but no one's dream date . . . why can't she find the right guy?

Molly – out for revenge against the four girls she has always been jealous of . . .

Emily – whose secure and happy life is about to be threatened by disaster.

Beth Rose – dreaming of love but wondering if it will ever become a reality.

Follow the five through their last years of high school, in four brilliant titles: *Saturday Night, Last Dance, New Year's Eve,* and *Summer Nights*

Caroline B. Cooney

[illegible]

[illegible]

[illegible]

[illegible]

[illegible]

[illegible]

[illegible]